THE WALK

Lee Goldberg

To Valerie & Madison

ACKNOWLEDGEMENTS

I want to thank William Rabkin and Tod Goldberg for their invaluable help in crafting this novel, and Ed Gorman for making it a reality.

CONTENTS

CHAPTER ONE
Sensurround

It wasn't like he imagined it at all. Of course, everything Martin Slack imagined seemed to come from television or movies, or at least big chunks of it, so he figured his own imagination really wasn't to blame for things not being the way they were supposed to be.

There weren't any of those ominous, early warning signs that everyone ignored, like big flocks of birds flying away or dogs barking for no reason, or the little rumbles that were shrugged off as a big truck passing by on the street.

Marty wasn't getting married, retiring from the force, embarking on a maiden voyage, or christening some bold, new construction project, each a definite precursor of disaster, at least according to Irwin Allen, the acknowledged expert on the subject.

And at least one thing turned out like the movies—here he was, underneath his car, just like Charlton Heston in *Earthquake*. That's where any similarity between Marty and Charlton ended.

He wasn't clutching Ava Gardner, and he certainly wouldn't sacrifice himself to save her over Genevieve Bujold. And after the shaking was over, Charlton wasn't curled in a fetal position, covered in dust and sprinkles of broken glass, wondering if the itchy wetness he felt on his legs was blood, something from the car, or his own piss.

Marty didn't want to move. He felt just like he did waking up in his soaked sleeping bag at Camp Cochise, afraid to stir, hoping everything would dry before the other campers, especially that bully Dwayne Edwards, woke up and discovered he was a bed-wetter. The sharpness of the fear and shame, thirty years later, surprised him almost as much as thinking about it now.

It was enough to embarrass him into opening his eyes and pushing away the bricks and broken glass that surrounded the car. He dragged himself from under his Mercedes, scraping his fingers on the shards of glass in his haste. But he didn't care. He had to get out.

The first thing he noticed was the dust, the chalky mist of pulverized plaster, mortar, and brick. It was everywhere. In his eyes, in his nose, in his lungs. Coughing, he staggered to his feet, his balance totally shot. It didn't help that asphalt was all cracked and bubbled, like something was trying to break out from underneath.

The derelict warehouse he'd been in just a few minutes before, making the obligatory network exec visit to the set of *Go to Heller*, was now just a pile of bricks, which slopped onto his car, flattening it like a $42,000 German beer can.

The warehouse was never retrofitted for earthquake safety. It had been abandoned and neglected for decades, which made it a great seedy location for cop shows.

But it wasn't abandoned today.

There were fifty or sixty people in there. The cast, the crew, the director. Now they were under tons of rubble. And if Marty had schmoozed ten seconds longer, he would have been, too.

Oh my God.

Marty stumbled over the debris, making his way around the edge of what had been the warehouse, and saw a handful of caterers, electricians, grips, and wardrobers swarming over the debris, quickly sorting through the bricks in a desperate search for survivors.

"Has anyone called for help?" he shouted, but didn't wait for an answer. He was already yanking out his cell phone, flipping it open like Capt. Kirk's communicator and dialing 911 as he approached them.

The tiny device bleated an electronic protest. No signal.

Shit!

What was the point of having a damn cell phone if you couldn't depend on it at times like this?

Marty snapped the phone shut, stuffed it into his pocket, and joined the others, picking up bricks and tossing them behind him as fast as he could.

This was really bad. A native Californian, Marty's ass was a natural Richter scale, accurate within two-tenths of a point. He knew the Northridge Quake was a 6.5 before CalTech did. And his ass was telling him this was bigger. Much bigger. Beyond the range of his experience.

"My brother," someone shrieked.

It was the guy beside Marty, one of the grips, the people who do the heavy lifting around the set. The guy was missing an ear, blood soaking his Panavision t-shirt from his shoulder down to his tool belt. But the guy was oblivious to it, he just kept repeating the same thing as he thrashed his way through the debris.

"My brother is in there," the guy said. "My brother is in there."

The guy said it over and over, becoming more frantic with each repetition. Marty focused on digging through the rubble directly in front of him. He didn't know what else to do.

Where the hell were the firemen? The police? Why wasn't he hearing any sirens?

"Over here!" one of the caterers yelled.

Everyone scrambled across the rubble toward the caterer, helping him heave the bricks aside, exposing first a bloody pant-leg, then a big, silver belt buckle.

That was all Marty needed to see. They'd found Irving Steinberg, the executive producer, a New York-born Jew who dressed like he was about to go on a cattle drive. Irving liked to refer to his ever-present Stetson as his "ten-gallon yarmulke."

In truth, Irving wore the Stetson because he thought it was less embarrassing and would draw less attention than even the most expensive toupee. Just look at Burt Reynolds and William Shatner, Irving would say. Wouldn't they look much better with hats?

Irving always made Marty smile. In fact, Marty was walking out with one of those Irving-produced smiles just before the rumbling started.

"Put this show on the fall schedule," Irving said, "and I can finally afford my dream."

"What's that?" Marty asked, willingly playing the straight man.

"My own ranch," Irving replied. "Right in Bel Air. I'm gonna call it the Bar Mitzvah spread."

They uncovered the rest of Irving.

If it wasn't for the trademark clothes, he would have been unrecognizable.

Marty backed away, shaking his head, struggling not to lose his balance as he fled. Irving was dead. Just a few minutes ago Irving was talking and joking and dreaming and now he was dead.

How could that be?

That's when someone jacked up the volume on the world. Suddenly Marty's ears opened up and he was bombarded by a shrill chorus of horns and car alarms, punctuated by the muffled rumble and pop of explosions, volleys on a distant battlefield.

Marty looked up.

It was like the theatre lights coming on after a movie, when he would notice the walls, the aisles, and the moviegoers he had forgotten were there. Now the lights were coming up on Marty's new world.

All the warehouses on the decaying, industrial block had either folded in on themselves in giant slabs or were reduced to rubble, all under a huge cloud of dust. The only structure still standing was a cardboard box mansion in the alley, its dirty-faced owner peeking out hesitantly at the destruction, then disappearing back inside, closing a flap behind him. His building was the only one on the block that seemed to be up to code.

Marty turned and saw the 6th Street bridge, the Art Deco giant slumped into the concrete banks of the LA river, pouring cars into the polluted dribble of water below. A big silver line of Metrolink rail cars had derailed, dangling over the vertical concrete embankment like decorative tinsel. Fire licked out of the windows, the flickering light shining off the dented, metal skin.

Marty turned again and saw the downtown LA skyline. Most of the glass towers still stood, like giant shattered mirrors, the harsh sun reflecting off their hideously cracked faces in jagged rays. They had swayed with the earth, as the engineers promised they would, shaking off their tinted glass skin. Only one high-rise couldn't hold on, and now leaned against another, as if too tired to stand any longer, panting smoke and flame in enormous bursts.

Marty turned and turned and turned, trying to take it all in. He couldn't. The enormity of the destruction was too much.

He felt an immediate distance, as if seeing it on a TV screen instead of living it. These were special effects, cardboard miniatures and plastic models. For a moment, he almost believed if he squinted, he could make out the matte lines between the real image and the computer-generated one painted in around it.

But he couldn't.

All of a sudden the ground started to heave. At first Marty thought it was an aftershock; then he realized it was himself, his whole body shaking violently. He fell to his knees and started to gag, vomiting until he thought he'd start spitting out organs.

Finally, the gagging stopped and Marty just stayed there, his eyes closed, waiting for his body to stop shaking, puke in his throat, in his nose. He found the horrible smell and sick taste strangely reassuring. It was something he recognized.

Marty straightened up and found a Kleenex in his pocket. He blew his nose, balled up the tissue, and tossed it.

Now he knew why he didn't hear sirens. Because no help was coming. Not for anyone. Not for a long time.

Time.

He'd left the warehouse set in a hurry, glancing at his watch as he rushed out, worried he'd be late for the staff meeting.

That was the last thing he did before it happened.

Now he looked at his watch again, a drop of blood landing on the cracked crystal just as he noted the time: 9:15 a.m. Tuesday.

7 :00 a.m. Tuesday
The radio report that woke Marty up predicted another day of sweltering heat and unhealthful air quality. Everyone was urged to stay indoors and avoid breathing too much.

Ordinarily, that wouldn't be a problem for him. He'd just go from the re-circulated air of his house to the re-circulated air of his car to the re-circulated air of his office with only seconds in between. But not today. He had to go downtown and make an appearance on the set.

Marty slapped the radio silent and didn't bother to look on the other side of the bed. He knew she'd already fled downstairs to the safety of the morning paper. Beth was always gone when he awoke, no matter what time it was.

It wasn't always that way.

They used to make love in the mornings, then lie tangled together, the sheets twisted around them, waiting for the radio alarm to go on and the chatty newscasters to drive them out of bed. Not any more.

He got up.

His house was above the smog, or at least he was high enough on the Calabasas hillside to enjoy the illusion that he was. From his bedroom window, he looked down onto the San Fernando Valley, at the thick, brown haze blanketing the flat urban sprawl. The layer of floating crud was trapped between the hills, which were slowly being devoured by tract homes like his. Only those homes cost about $300,000 less and were crammed onto a mere 6000-square-foot patch of dry graded dirt. They were stucco boxes for the Camry class.

Marty shifted his gaze to the red-tile roof of the Spanish colonial guard house and the morning progression of gardeners and pool cleaners and housekeepers climbing up the steep hill of his gated community in their over-loaded pick-ups and dented cars. He wondered if they knew they weren't supposed to breathe today.

He trudged naked into the bathroom, and as he stood urinating into the toilet, reminded himself of all the things on his schedule. First, visit the set of *Go to Heller*, a supernatural pilot about a dead cop who rises from the grave and becomes a private eye.

Marty's plan was to shake a few hands and pretend the network was wildly enthusiastic about the footage they were seeing, then rush back to the office for the weekly staff meeting where, as the guy in charge of current programming, he was responsible for the creative direction of the network's shows.

Standards & Practices was in an uproar over the nipplage in the romantic adventure series *Sam and Sally*. Seeing erect nipples under clothing once in an hour was considered an acceptable accident. Twice was salacious. Three times was offensive content. They wanted Sally to start taping herself down. Marty was adamantly against it.

In the shower, under the hottest spray he could endure, he considered the various ways he could argue his point. He could try and shame them: Nipples are a fact of life. We all have them. What are we trying to hide here? It's not like she's running around topless. It was ludicrous to demand that an actress "restrain her aggressive nipples" so some tight-ass censor could pretend women didn't have them.

Or he could take the artistic, pragmatic approach. More and more viewers are fleeing the artificially chaste world of network television for the more realistic programming on pay-cable, where nudity, sex, and profanity are commonplace. If they are going to successfully compete, they have to be less puritanical in their thinking.

Or he could try the truth. The only reason anybody watched *Sam and Sally* was to see Sally's nipples. And if she taped them down, they might at well cancel the show.

As Marty slipped into his beige pants, white shirt, and navy blue dark jacket, he decided to go with the truth, if only to see that standards prick Adam Horsting turn pale.

He headed for the stairs, pausing for a moment to look in the kid's room. They didn't have a kid, but they had the room. For some reason, he just couldn't pass the open door without looking in. Stuffed animals with permanent, vacant stares looked at him between the slats of the empty crib. We're waiting.

Marty went back and closed the door, but he knew it would be open by the time he got home. He hurried down the stairs and into the kitchen with an enthusiasm he didn't feel.

Beth was sitting at the kitchen table in her bathrobe, leaning over the LA Times and a cup of coffee, her bare feet entwined in the fur of their sleeping dog, Max. The fat golden retriever delighted in being her ottoman. It was one of two things Max was good at. The other was the ability to pick the most expensive shoes Marty owned to chew on. Max obviously liked the taste of Italian leather.

His wife had short blond hair, bright blue eyes, and a band of freckles across her nose that made her look like a mischievous child. People thought she was cute, and she hated that. She was certain it meant that no one took her seriously.

"Good morning," He said, sticking his head in the pantry, looking for something he could eat on the run.

"They found a shark with a mouth that glows in the dark," she said. "It got caught in a fisherman's net. They think it's some unknown species that lives in the deepest, darkest part of the ocean."

"Uh-huh." He peered into an open box of Cinnamon Pop Tarts. There was one foil package left inside. That would hold him until he could swipe some fruit off the craft services table on the set.

"They think the shark swims with his mouth open. The light attracts the fish and they swim right down his throat," she flipped through the pages, scanning the headlines. "They think there could be lots of species down there we've never seen."

"Sounds like there could be a series in that." He stuck the foil pack in his pocket and went to the refrigerator, where he snagged a can of Coke, absently knocking something on the floor. "Though the last successful underwater show was thirty years ago."

"The whole world doesn't revolve around television." Beth said, followed by one of her dismissive sighs.

"Most people wouldn't know what they wanted to eat, what they wanted to wear, or who they wanted to fuck if the TV didn't tell them," he bent down to pick up whatever he dropped. "So as vice president of current drama, I obviously play a vital role in our society."

Marty smiled to let her know he was joking, or at least being delightfully self-deprecating.

"You dropped something," she motioned to the floor with a slight nod of her head.

It was a tiny vial. He picked it up. Pergonal. It had expired months ago. He was about to throw it out when he saw her staring at him. So instead Marty hastily put the vial back in the refrigerator and slammed the door, as if the vial might fight its way out again. The last thing he wanted to do was resurrect The Discussion.

When Marty turned around, he was relieved to see she was reading her paper again. He popped the top on the Coke and took a big gulp, studying her over the top of the can as he swallowed. She was especially lovely in the morning, hair tussled, face still flushed with the warmth of sleep.

Beth seemed to sense his eyes on her and the affection behind them. "Are you going to be late tonight?" she asked softly.

"I should be back before primetime." That used to make her smile, a hundred repetitions ago.

And then, as if reading his thoughts, she gave him a small smile and returned to her paper.

9:16 a.m. Tuesday
Marty sat on his Richter scale, picking bloody bits of glass out of his hair as he wondered what the hell he should do.

It wasn't supposed to happen like this. He wasn't supposed to be here.

In all his earthquake scenarios, he was always at home, where he was fully prepared. Everything in the house was bolted, strapped, or stuck down. There was bag under the bed bulging with survivalist stuff?bought in a binge after the last quake. There was even a sack of food for the dog. And on the slim chance the house was decimated, they had camping gear in the garage for emergency shelter.

At least he knew that Beth was safe.

If the house didn't collapse on her.

There was nothing to worry about, he told himself. They had a thorough geological survey done when they bought the house. The report said it was earthquake safe and built on solid bedrock.

Yeah, and the house inspector said the drainage was great and what happened the first time it really rained? Water flooded the yard, seeped under the French doors, and ruined the hardwood floors. Remember?

He had to go home.

But how?

He was stuck in downtown LA, a decaying urban wilderness, thirty miles from the safety of his gated community in Calabasas, his Mercedes crushed. And even if it wasn't, the roads and freeways were going to be all but impassable for any vehicle.

He'd have to walk.

No easy feat for a guy who's idea of a long walk was from the couch to the TV set, but he could do it. He had no choice, unless he wanted to stay here. And he knew what happened to guys like him who took a wrong turn and ended up in the 'hood alone, looking white, rich, and privileged, armed with only a spring-loaded Mercedes key-fob.

His heart started to race. He thought he might begin gagging again. He took a deep breath and willed himself to focus.

Marty looked back at his E-class. The trunk, defiantly shiny and unscratched, pinched out from under the rubble. He hurried over to the car, popped open the trunk, and rooted around the piles of scripts and videos until he found an old LA street map. Then he grabbed his gym bag, which was wedged into the furthest corner. It had been six months since he used the bag, back when he was caught up in the early enthusiasm of a new year's resolution and a two-year gym membership. He went twice and never went back.

Inside the gym bag were a pair of old Reeboks, a t-shirt, some sweats, and a bottle of water. He shoved the tire iron, a flashlight, and the Mercedes first-aid kit into the bag.

It was a start.

As he kicked off his stiff dress shoes and put on the Reeboks, he started thinking about what else he'd need for his journey. Packaged food, lots of water, duct tape, matches, dust masks, some rope. Basically, he had to make a mini-version of his home survival kit.

No problem. He could find most of those things right here, between the catering wagon, wardrobe trailer, and the grip, prop, and lighting trucks. Film crews had everything.

All he needed now was a plan of action.

Marty figured there was maybe nine hours of summer daylight left. If he started walking now, even as out of shape as he was, he could easily be in the valley and heading down Ventura Boulevard by nightfall.

That was okay.

He certainly had nothing to fear in the valley, where Tarzan and Universal Studios had entire communities named after them and the oldest historical landmark was the Casa De Cadillac dealership.

All he had to figure out now was the best way to get there.

It was possible to live your entire life in Los Angeles and never see the bad parts of town, except in a seventy-mile-per-hour blur on the freeway or channel-flipping past the evening news on the way to a *Cheers* rerun.

Even so, Marty knew where those dangerous neighborhoods were, and he was well aware that to get home, he'd have to walk through some of them. There was no way around it.

But he tried to make himself feel better by looking at the bright side. He'd be walking in broad daylight, in the midst of chaos, and would only be in truly bad places for a few miles. There were far worse parts of the city he could be stuck in. At least he wasn't visiting Compton, or South Central, when the quake hit.

He slammed the trunk shut and spread the yellowed, torn street map out on top of it. Calabasas was on the south-western edge of the San Fernando Valley, on the other side of the Santa Monica

Mountains and the Hollywood Hills.

There were two major freeways into the valley, the 101 over the Cahuenga Pass just five or ten miles north of downtown, or the 405 through the Sepulveda Pass, a good fifteen miles or twenty miles west. Between the two passes, there were three major canyon roads that snaked over the Hollywood Hills.

The other option was to head due west to the beaches of Santa Monica and then follow the Pacific Coast Highway north to one of the canyon roads that cut through the Santa Monica Mountains. But that meant crossing the entire LA basin, which was the last thing Marty wanted to do.

He decided the quickest, safest way home was the way he'd come, taking the 101, better known as the Hollywood Freeway, northwest over the Cahuenga Pass into the valley.

That was assuming there were no major obstacles in his path. Which, of course, there would be. Toppled buildings, buckled roads, crumpled freeways.

But that wasn't what worried him.

It was the thousands of little obstacles. The people. The injured and the dead underneath it all. The earthquake's human debris.

Then there were the derelicts and gang-bangers, who he hoped would be too busy looting to pay attention to one man walking home.

He wouldn't look at anyone. He'd just hurry along. Gone before anyone noticed him.

Just keep walking. Across the city, over the hills, and along the valley, never stopping until he got to his front door, where his wife would be waiting, alive and well.

Simple. From point A to point B.

Not too complicated. No reason he couldn't do it. There were guys who walked across entire states in the frontier days. Or at least they did in the western novels his flunkies read and summarized for him.

Marty zipped up the bag and headed for the trucks and trailers to assemble his kit.

He was going home.

CHAPTER TWO
On the Yellow Brick Road

10:30 a.m. Tuesday

Marty emerged from the grip truck, ready to go, his bulging gym bag looped over his shoulders like a backpack.

He pulled a white paper dust mask over his nose and mouth, slipped on his Ray-bans, took a deep, filtered breath, and headed off.

It meant going past the rubble of the warehouse again. The surviving crewmembers were too intent on their work to notice Marty, which is what he was hoping. He diverted his gaze, afraid someone would see him watching and try to draft him into the hopeless enterprise.

The three bodies the surviving crewmembers had recovered so far were laid out on the cracked asphalt under the tent that was supposed to protect the caterer's junk food from the sun. It was amazing the tent was still standing. But the table had fallen, the donuts, candy, fruit, and drinks splattered on the street in a swath of crushed ice.

A woman Marty recognized as one of the hairdressers sobbed beside the body of Clarissa Blake, one of the twenty-something stars of the show. The hairdresser was soaking a napkin with Evian, trying to wipe the blood and dirt off Clarissa's unnaturally pale face, the only part of her celebrated body that was still identifiable. It was as if someone placed a perfect Clarissa Blake mask on a deflated inflatable girl. Thinking of it like that, it didn't seem real any more, just a grotesque rubber prop on a horror movie set.

Again, he glanced away quickly, not wanting to be drawn into the morbid scene or think too deeply about it. Clarissa Blake was dead, nothing Marty could do to change that. And bottled water was far too valuable now to be wasting on cleaning the dead. It could be days, maybe weeks, before drinking water was easy to come by.

The thought made Marty swoop down and grab a couple Evians off the ground, jamming them into his jacket pockets as he went. The little bottles were still cold.

Marty walked up the middle of Sante Fe Avenue, wanting to put as much distance between himself and anything that could collapse on him as possible. The most important thing now was to avoid tall buildings and power lines, tunnels and overpasses, staying out in the open as much as possible, even if it meant veering a mile or two off-course. It would be really stupid if he survived the quake only to get squashed by chunk of concrete two minutes later.

Marty didn't know downtown LA well; in fact, he probably hadn't been here more than half-a-dozen times in ten years, but he'd seen it from the sky, flying into LAX from New York or Hawaii. From above, the skyscrapers looked like a tangle of weeds breaking through a crack in a parking lot. It wouldn't be hard to keep away from them. He'd head north, cut across the Civic Center on 1st Street, then follow the course of the Hollywood Freeway back into the valley.

Having a solid plan, and a gym bag full of emergency supplies, made him feel in control of the situation. It was a relief to know that the shifting tectonic plates of the earth's crust could be tamed by clear thinking, bottled spring water, and a Thomas Brothers map.

There usually wasn't much traffic on Sante Fe any more, an industrial neighborhood with no more industry. So there were only a few cars on the street now, spread haphazardly along the roadway, banged-up Hot Wheels thrown on the floor by a bored child ready to play something else.

Marty approached a Crown Vic, resting on its side on a jagged slab of bulging asphalt, its wheels spinning slowly. The obese, middle-aged driver was still alive, belted into his seat and wide-eyed with shock, resting his head on the blood-speckled airbag like a pillow, listening to the radio.

"They're dead . . . they're all dead. There's fire everywhere. I can't get out. Harvey . . . he's burning. He's behind the glass and he's burning. He's all on fire. Oh, God. Oh, shit. If he doesn't stop banging against the glass, it's going to break! Stop! Can't you see it's cracking? Stop! Goddamn it, Harvey! Please!"

The driver didn't seem to hear it, or if he did, he was mistaking it for soothing music. Marty wasn't blessed with such blissful delusions. The terror was seeping out of the radio's speakers like smoke and he didn't want to breathe it.

He kept right on walking past the car, trying not to listen to the frantic newscaster and yet unable to stop himself.

"Oh God, it's fucking breaking! Oh God. Oh fuck. I don't want to die! Somebody help me!"

Marty quickened his pace, stumbling over cracks and rocks, until he couldn't hear the voice any more, the newscaster's pleading muffled by the sobbing, moaning, and cries of pain coming from a parking lot up ahead.

Several dozen workers were behind a wrought-iron fence topped with curls of razor wire, huddled as far as they could get from the building they'd just escaped, its pre-fab concrete walls caving in under a collapsed roof. They hugged each other, covered in plaster and gore, lost in their sorrow and fear.

Don't look, Marty told himself. Keep moving.

He knew there were going to be a lot more sights like this. Dioramas on a gruesome theme park ride. He couldn't let any of them get to him. The only person he had to care about was Beth. That was his moral imperative as a good husband.

So he was absolutely doing the right thing. Letting himself get distracted from his moral imperative by the misery of others would be the real sin.

Up ahead, the 4th Street bridge arched over Sante Fe Avenue on its way across the LA River to Boyle Heights. The concrete bridge was still standing, unlike its big sister two blocks south, but as Marty got closer, he could see it was severely cracked, raining a fine powder on the street. Perhaps it was only cosmetic damage, but it wasn't worth the risk.

Marty took the first side street that came along. It wasn't much wider than an alley, bordered by gutted, decomposing factories, and blocked mid-way through by an ugly car accident. A big-rig truck had driven over one of those boxy old Volvos, then rolled over and slammed through the wall of a derelict loading dock.

His best guess was that the two vehicles were about to pass one another in the instant before the quake and veered head-on at each other.

He stopped for a moment, worried, feeling beads of sweat roll down his back.

What was bothering him?

There was no fire, and if he hugged the sidewalk on the opposite side of the street, he could slip past the accident easily and continue on to Alameda Street, where he was bound to see worse pile-ups than this.

Much worse. And just think about what the Harbor Freeway is going to look like, he told himself. You're going to have to cross that soon enough. This is nothing.

He braced himself for the worst and pushed on, his own footsteps sounding unnaturally loud, crunching on bits of glass and crumbs of concrete. The air smelled of mulch, like a freshly planted garden, even through his perspiration-soaked dust mask.

As he edged past the accident, he couldn't help looking at the carnage. Every Los Angeleno had the same, undeniable urge; it was why even an overheated Chevette parked on the freeway shoulder could cause a traffic snarl going back twenty miles.

The cab of the truck was imbedded in the warehouse, sparing him the sight of the driver. The cargo trailer was cracked open, spilling bags of potting soil, which had burst open on impact, spraying dark black dirt everywhere. Now he knew where the smell came from.

The Volvo was squashed nearly flat and covered in dirt. Even the dullest, safest car made was no match for a Mack truck. The two vehicles bled gasoline, oil, and coolant, which pooled against the curb near Marty's feet.

Something crackled.

He peered over the Volvo and saw a severed electrical line jerking on the ground, spitting sparks. The truck had taken down a power-pole across the street. The live wire was far away from him and the leaking gasoline. Even so, he would be glad to put some distance between himself and the power line, which he eyed as if it were a living thing, a predator waiting to attack.

And that's when something *did*, grabbing him by the ankle.

He screamed and instinctively tried to jump away, tripping himself and hitting the ground hard, provoking another scream, only this one wasn't his own. It was a scream of agony from inside the car.

Marty scrambled away, looking back to see a dirt-caked arm sticking out of the Volvo, clutching desperately at the air. It was like a hand shooting out of a grave.

"Help me, please," a woman's voice pleaded from inside the crumpled Volvo.

He could run. Just keep going. No one would ever know.

"I can't breathe," she whimpered.

Marty was crawling to the car before he was even aware he'd made a decision, taking her hand and peering into the opening it came from. It was as if he were staring in the mouth of some metal monster, a great white Volvo that was chewing this poor young woman alive. The lower half of her body was completely consumed by jagged metal, her upper body nearly buried in potting soil. Her other arm was twisted at an unnatural angle, ragged splinters of bone ripping through the skin.

"Hold on," Marty said, "I'm right here."

He reached in and scooped the dirt away, clearing her head so she could breathe. She had hair almost as dark as the soil, and green eyes that blazed with terrified intensity. She took in the air with shallow, raspy breaths.

"I thought you were going to leave me." Her voice was tinged with a slight Texas twang. He guessed she was about thirty.

Marty took off his glasses and pulled his dust mask down from his face, leaving it hanging around his neck. "You startled me. That's all."

He almost asked if she was all right before he caught himself. The question was a stupid reflex. She was obviously in deep, deep trouble. Even though her blouse was covered with dirt, he could see it was drenched with blood, oozing where the car was gnashing her.

"Is there anybody else with you?" he asked.

16

"No, thank God," she licked the blood from her lips and looked up at him with pleading eyes. "Can you get me out of here?"

Her body and the metal were meshed tightly together. There was no way he could do anything, not with just his hands and a tiny tire-iron. It would take a team of firemen, the jaws-of-life, and some paramedics. And even then, he had his doubts.

"I don't think so," he replied. "And I'm afraid of what would happen if I tried."

She nodded slightly. "It's okay. I think I already knew the answer anyway. Can you do anything for the truck driver?"

"I don't know," Marty glanced away, surprised by the sudden stab of guilt he felt. When he glanced back, she was looking at him strangely.

"Maybe you should check."

The way she said it, without being overtly judgmental or scornful, somehow made it sound even more damning. He started to get up and she grabbed him again, gently this time.

"You'll come back, right?" she asked.

"Yeah," he said, "Of course I will."

Marty got to his feet and went to the truck. Fifteen minutes into his journey and already he was breaking the rules. If he were smart, he would keep on walking. There was nothing he could do for her.

As he neared the truck, he kept his eye on the fallen live wire, undulating on the pavement, hissing and crackling. The puddle of gasoline was still far away from the sparks, but that could change.

He climbed up the side of the cab and looked down through the driver's side window. At first, he couldn't make sense of what he was seeing. The driver was slumped against the passenger door, but his head was in his lap. How could that be?

An instant later, his mind registered what he saw. A sheet of corrugated metal, ripped from the warehouse wall on impact, had chopped through the windshield like an ax, lopping off the driver's head.

Marty scrambled off the cab as if decapitation was infectious, backing away without taking his eyes off the wreckage, just waiting for some new horror to pop up.

When Marty was eight years old, he stepped on a nail and it went right through his foot. Up until now, that was the worst physical injury he'd ever witnessed, if he didn't count Irving

Steinberg and Clarissa Blake.

He backed right into the Volvo, causing it to rock, the woman's cry of pain snapping him out of it. The woman, somehow he had to help the woman. Who was he kidding? There wasn't a damn thing he could do for her. This was a job for professionals.

Marty reached inside his jacket for his cell phone and tried to dial 911. Once again, he couldn't get a signal. But even if he could, what were the chances anybody would come for her with a city in ruins? She'd be the very last priority.

There was only him. And Marty didn't have the slightest idea what to do. He fought back the urge to run, shoved the phone back into his jacket, and crouched beside the car again.

"How is he?" she asked, but interrupted him before he could speak. "Never mind, I can see it on your face."

She shuddered, grimacing in agony. He had never seen anyone go through such pain before and he didn't want to see it now. He looked away. Blood trickled from her nose and escaped from the corners of her mouth.

"My name is Molly," she whispered. "Molly Hobart."

"Marty Slack." He took a Kleenex from his pocket and wiped the blood off her face, then wondered what to do with the tissue afterward. What if she had AIDS? He dropped the tissue and hoped none of the blood got on his hands. "Is there anything I can do to make you more comfortable?"

There was a first aid kit in his gym bag, but he doubted a squirt of Bactine and an ouch-less Band-Aid were going to make her feel any better.

"Just hold my hand and talk to me," Molly said, "until help gets here."

That could be days, if it ever came at all.

Marty couldn't stay and wait. He was on his way home. If he didn't get into the valley by nightfall, he could be in real danger. She'd understand that. All he had to do was tell her and she'd let him go.

"Sure," he said.

"Could I have some water?"

He took one of the bottles out of his pocket, twisted off the cap, and poured a little Evian slowly into her mouth. She was having a hard time swallowing.

After a moment, she said softly: "I'm not supposed to be here."

"I know what you mean," he said.

"No, really. It's wrong. There's a body shop near my house I could have gone there. But the bastard insurance company said I had to get the car fixed at this place downtown, or they wouldn't pay for it. That's not right, is it?"

"What happened?"

"My daughter spilled grape juice on the seat. I reached back to grab the box of Kleenex before it got all over everything and sideswiped a parked car," Molly squeezed his hand, tentatively, like she was checking if it was still there. "Two accidents in one month. They're really going to jack up my rates now."

"No one's going to blame you for this."

"You haven't met my insurance company," she said. "Has anyone called 911 yet?"

"I tried, but I can't get a signal."

"I'm sure someone has called."

In that instant, he had a sickening realization. Molly had no idea what happened to her, what really caused her accident. And if he told her, she'd know just how little her predicament mattered to anyone right now.

Anyone but him.

He should have gone under the bridge, cracked or not. He should have just said a prayer and run as fast as he could.

"You're from Texas," Marty said.

"Thalia," she replied. "It's a real small town."

"What brought you to LA?"

"Another accident," Molly smiled, her teeth smeared with blood. "Clara's five years old now." She let go of his hand and pointed to the sun visor. "Pull that down."

Marty did. There was a photo pinned to the visor with a rubber band. He slid it out and looked at it.

It was a picture of Molly, a radiant smile on her face, a smaller version of herself in her lap, the two of them on a picnic blanket on a lush lawn somewhere. The kid was maybe five, old enough to know how to pose adorably for a camera.

"My whole life has been a series of accidents," Molly said, "Clara is the only one that made me happy."

Clara even made Molly smile now, entwined in metal, holding hands with a stranger. The thought of a child made Molly smile as easily as it made Beth break into tears.

"Do you have children?" she asked.

"No," he replied. "We tried for a while, but it didn't take."

For months, Marty snuck away from the network for "power lunches" at a Beverly Hills fertility clinic, masturbating into a cup in their tastefully appointed hospitality rooms. At first, it wasn't so bad. There were worse ways to spend a lunch hour than jerking off with an X-rated DVD.

But one day he stepped from his hospitality room with his sample cup and bumped into Freddie Koslow, a studio development guy, coming out of the hospitality room next door. The two infertile executives stood there, holding their cups of sperm, casually discussing projects in development as if they'd just bumped into each other at the Bistro Garden.

That was the last time Marty visited the clinic. But he didn't tell any of this to Molly. It was bad enough half the television industry knew about his shiftless sperm.

"We weren't trying for anything except some fun," Molly said. "We did it just once, and that was all it took. Roy disappeared right away, and I couldn't stay in Thalia, not like that. So I left before she was born. I was heading for San Francisco, but the car broke down as I was passing through LA. So I stayed. See? Another accident."

Molly's face suddenly crunched into an agonized wince, her eyes closed tight, squeezing out tears of pain. She reached out and grabbed his wrist, squeezing it hard, digging her fingers into his skin until he had to stifle a cry of his own.

Her grip eased, and when she opened her eyes again, he saw just how scared she was. No amount of talking was going to distract her now.

"She's at Dandelion Preschool in Tarzana," Molly said in a rush, "you'll call the school from the hospital, let them know what happened?"

"Sure," he said.

And then Marty heard it, the unmistakable rumble, like a stomach growling below his feet. Molly's eyes went wide.

"What is it?" she cried out in that one, hanging instant before the inevitable.

"Aftershock!" he yelled.

"Aftershock?"

Marty realized his mistake too late, and just as he saw the betrayal and confusion registering on her face, the shaking started, the giant, unseen waves rolling under the street.

He gripped Molly's hand tight, tucked his head down, and closed his eyes to ride it out. The rumbling grew louder, the subterranean thunder mixing with the sounds of concrete cracking, glass breaking, metal grinding. The two wrecked vehicles rocked back and forth, creaking like rusty hinges. The car slid away, jerking her hand from his grasp.

Marty reached out for her again, but was driven back into a fetal curl by falling masonry that shattered on impact, exploding into dusty shrapnel that pierced his skin in tiny pin-pricks.

And then it was over. The rumbling receding like a fleeing stampede.

Marty unfurled slowly, stinging all over, and surveyed the damaged. The Volvo had slid a few feet, and so had the truck, gasoline gushing out of its ruptured tank and surging towards the live wire dancing on the street.

He ran to the car and leaned into it. Molly stared up at him with desperate eyes, one hand reaching out to him, blood gurgling out of her mouth, drowning the words she tried to speak.

She was trapped and so was Marty, confined by a few dwindling seconds, forced to choose between her plight and his own survival.

Marty looked from her to the wire. The fingers of gasoline were only a few inches from contact with the wire. He had seconds.

Molly grabbed him, pulling him down.

He whirled around, and for one horrified moment, thought he'd have to fight Molly off to escape. But she immediately let go, opening her hand to show him the picture she clutched in her palm, offering it to him, her eyes pleading.

"I'm sorry," he whispered, and ran.

He heard her yell one, last, desperate time, something that sounded like "Angel," and then the truck erupted behind him, the force of it lifting him off his feet and hurling him onto Alameda Street, the fireball rolling over his head.

Marty hit the pavement face-first, too hard and too fast to do anything to break his fall, knocking the air out of him, crushing his glasses and smashing one of the tiny water bottles in his jacket pocket. As he lay gasping for breath, a piece of paper fluttered in front of his face, tiny flames beginning to curl the edges. It was the picture of Molly's kid. He slapped the flames out with his hand.

The edges of the picture were charred, but the smiling faces were intact. The Molly in the photo and the woman he'd left behind, the woman with the pleading eyes and bloody smile, were two different people. Marty would never be able to reconcile the two images, one of which he knew he would never shake.

Angel.

Was she crying out to her daughter, her little angel, with that last breath? Or was she calling out to Marty, mistaking him in her desperation for something he definitely was not? Or was she screaming in horrified recognition at the dark spirit that came to take her away?

He'd never know, but he'd probably never stop wondering, either.

Marty took the photo and staggered to his feet. Every part of his body seemed to ache. His hair was singed, his face was scratched, one pant-leg was torn at the knee, and his crotch was soaked with Evian, but he'd made it.

He turned slowly towards the narrow street, staring at the sight in disbelief. Both vehicles were engulfed in flames, the fire spreading to the ruins of the nearby buildings.

If he'd hesitated another second, he would have been burned alive. That's how close he cut it.

Up until today, he managed to live his life without risking it even once. And now, twice in one morning, he'd barely avoided death.

That kind of luck doesn't last, not for real people. He was almost killed, all because he stopped, all because he let himself be pulled into someone else's problem. Molly's certain death nearly became his.

He wouldn't make that mistake again.

Marty turned his back to the fire, crammed the picture deep into his wet pocket, adjusted the straps of the gym bag over his shoulders, and started walking.

CHAPTER THREE
This is the City, Los Angeles, California

11:40 a.m. Tuesday
Marty's Ray-Bans teetered precariously on the bridge of his nose, held in place by only one arm. A lens was cracked, too, but there was no way he was taking the glasses off. They were part of his disguise as he moved purposefully up the middle of Alameda Street, carefully winding his way through the debris field of fractured pavement, smashed cars, and crumpled buildings.

His dust mask was crushed, but he molded it back into shape and pulled it up over his nose and mouth. He only had three masks left and wasn't disposing of this one until it absolutely couldn't be used any more. It also covered his face and helped conceal any sympathy or fear that might inadvertently escape.

Smoke and dust filled the air, shrouding him in a swirling fog of destruction. He welcomed it. The haze further obscured him from others and they from him.

He ignored the crashed cars and the crushed cars and the victims inside them.

He ignored the dazed survivors, most of them elderly Asians, stumbling across his path like drunks, their faces lined and puckered with age.

He ignored the injured and the dead, laid out on the sidewalks like garage sale trinkets on display.

And he ignored the crying, the moaning, and the screaming.

He ignored it all.

There were a thousand Mollys out there, and he didn't want to meet another one. It was too painful and far too dangerous.

Marty kept his gaze at his feet, following the twisted iron of the long-forgotten railroad track imbedded in the broken asphalt. Or maybe it was an old trolley track. Marty didn't know and didn't really care. What little Los Angeles history he knew was gleaned from *Dragnet* reruns. If Jack Webb didn't film it, Marty didn't know it.

He didn't feel he was missing anything. Los Angeles didn't have much history anyway and what little it did have was paved over the instant it showed any age, which made sense to him. The only buildings tourists cared about were ones they saw repeatedly on TV or in classic movies, and most of those were facades on studio back-lots. In that regard, he was a learned historian.

Stately Wayne Manor. The Bates Motel. Melrose Place. 77 Sunset Strip. Baywatch headquarters. Jed Clampett's mansion. The Brady's house. Gilligan's lagoon. Cabot Cove. These places were more culturally and emotionally meaningful to LA, and perhaps to most people born after 1950, than the weedy battlefields of Gettysburg, the Liberty Bell, or the White House itself.

Beyond TV and film locations, the most interesting and significant landmarks in the city were as transitory and disposable as the historical record they were printed on—the slim "Maps to the Stars' Homes" distributed by bored Latinos sitting on folding beach chairs at street corners and freeway off-ramps.

Now they would all have to be replaced by new landmarks.

Marty was passing through Little Tokyo, a fact he wouldn't have known if the blue sign demarcating the neighborhood wasn't still standing, canted at a right angle. Now he noticed the Japanese businesses, their signs dangling from crumbling storefronts, or lying broken on the streets. Landwa Food. Mitsuwa Marketplace. Yaohan Plaza. And even through the dust, he could smell the unmistakably salty, greasy, and fishy aroma of Japanese food.

Or perhaps it was just Marty's imagination, spurred by the pained and perplexed Asian faces, the indecipherable Japanese lettering, the knowledge he was in their tiny, dying corner of a fading urban center.

The railroad track veered off and disappeared into a parking lot on the northwestern corner of 2nd and Alameda. Hundreds of terrified people gathered on the uneven concrete clearing, staring at the buildings they'd escaped from, taking comfort in the arms of their friends and co-workers, the agonized wailing of all those jostled cars drowning out their own.

He moved on, past a pile of sooty brick, rusted iron bars, and corroded metal awnings, all that remained of an abandoned building that had dissolved like a sugar cube hit by a drop of water. A bewildered security guard, presumably there to protect the place from squatters, sat on a stool in his rickety plywood shack, which was barely larger than the man himself. Judging from the look on the guard's face, Marty guessed he wouldn't be leaving his tall, narrow shelter any time soon.

The face of the Japanese American Museum had disintegrated, a pile of shattered glass glittering like snow in the wide plaza at Alameda and 1st Street. Marty crossed the intersection and headed west.

Even without a sign, he would've known he was in Little Tokyo now. On the south side of the street, a recreation of a wooden watchtower marked the entrance to a mini-mall designed to resemble an authentic Japanese village, at least as it would have been if built by a Winchell's Donuts franchisee.

The center, or what was left of it, faced a block of historic buildings dating back to the 1880s and the first Japanese settlers, something Marty wouldn't have known if he wasn't watching where he stepped. The previous occupants of the buildings, from the 1800s up until World War II, were inscribed in brass letters in the broken, buckled sidewalk as part of some urban art project.

Marty stopped in front of one of the buildings and read the listing: 1890, Queen Hotel. 1910, Nihon Hotel. 1914, T. Kato, Midwife. 1926, Dr. W. Tsukifuji, Dentist. 1935, Ushikawa Hospital. Now it was a video store.

A few steps farther down was Fugetsu Do, the Japanese bakery where the first fortune cookie was created. Marty looked through the shattered window. No one was inside. Perhaps the baker got advance warning from one of his cookies.

Marty continued on, Little Tokyo abruptly giving way to the

Civic Center. A sign outside of City Hall announced that the 28-story edifice, familiar to anyone who ever looked at an LA policeman's badge, was undergoing an extensive seismic retrofitting that obviously came too late. The imposing, phallic tower, thrusting a faux-Greek temple into the heavens, was the official symbol of the city and it was even more so now, snapped in half, lying across the park like a fallen soldier.

But across the street, the ramshackle "World Famous Home of the Authentic Kosher Mexican Burrito" withstood the quake unscathed and was open for business. Steam escaped from the tiny, open kitchen, where the perspiring chef, seemingly oblivious to the disaster, was busily serving meals to the equally oblivious customers at the sidewalk counter.

If Marty limited his view to just the burrito stand, it looked like just another lunch hour, the counter crowded with hungry paralegals, secretaries, and civil servants, munching over-stuffed burritos and chugging huge sodas. The only thing wrong with the picture was that everyone was bleeding from somewhere, their clothes ripped, their bodies covered with dust. But there was no panic here, no moaning, no sobbing. The customers seemed to take great comfort in their familiar burritos, keeping their gaze on the kitchen and away from the shaken world around them.

Without thinking, Marty abruptly turned and headed for the burrito stand. Even though he hated Mexican food, he suddenly had an overpowering urge for a burrito; he didn't know why. Perhaps it was astonishment that drew him, the discovery of an oasis in the disaster. Then again, he'd never tried a Kosher burrito before, and this was certainly the day for new experiences.

Marty shouldered his way to the counter, pulled down his dust mask, and filled his nostrils with the smell of sizzling fat. Faded, water-stained photos of direct-to-video movie stars and TV character actors hung on the walls, their sun-bleached autographs retraced with a ball-point pen by a shaky hand. Lee Horsley ate here. A place couldn't have a stronger recommendation than that.

The chef worked frantically, taking orders, serving food, and running the cash register.

"What would you like?" The chef asked with a heavy, Mexican accent.

Marty glanced up at the menu. Besides the Kosher Burrito, and a dozen variations on it, they offered Teriyaki Chicken Burritos for their Japanese neighbors, hamburgers for the bland bureaucrat, and Shrimp Cocktails for the discerning gourmet. What would Lee Horsley have chosen?

"What's a Kosher Burrito?" Marty asked.

"Pastrami, Hebrew National salami, corned beef, chili sauce, onions, mustard, pickles and peppers wrapped in a home-made tortilla," the chef replied. "Is very very good."

All that was missing was a matzo ball and gefilte fish to really make it work.

"I'll take it," Marty put four dollars on the counter. "And a coke."

The chef swept the money into his hand, dumped it in the open register, and returned to his cooking, digging a handful of chopped meat out of a bucket and tossing it onto the hissing grill. Marty watched him.

"You know there was an earthquake, right?" Marty asked.

The chef replied without turning around. "People still got to eat. I still got to make a living."

Marty was about to ask what inspired the chef to create such a bizarre entrée, but was distracted by a hard shove from the big guy next to him.

"Hey asshole, your back is on fire."

Marty looked over his shoulder and, out of the corner of his eye, saw smoke rising from his gym bag. He yelped, shrugged the bag off and dropped it on the concrete floor, stomping out the flames. It was only after the fire was smothered, and he was staring down breathlessly at the scorched bag, that he realized the stupidity of what he'd done.

He'd put out the fire and saved the bag, only to destroy anything that hadn't burned inside by stomping on it. If he'd bothered to think first, instead of panicking, he could have extinguished the flames with a little water.

Now he knew why there was so much smoke everywhere he went.

"Nice going, dumbfuck." The big guy beside him, wearing the JC Penney suit and Wal-Mart tie, guffawed mightily, skillfully avoiding choking on a mouthful of burrito at the same time.

Marty picked up his burned bag and carried it over to one of the wobbly tables, where he spilled out the contents on the chipped Formica top.

The transistor radio was smashed, and so was the flashlight, but Marty thought he still might be able to get it to work. A couple of his Evian bottles had broken open, soaking his matches, but they would dry out. Or at least he hoped they would. His t-shirt was scorched, and so were a few of his granola bars, but the duct tape, first aid kit, and most of the other stuff seemed to be okay.

"You thought you were prepared for The Big One, didn't you, Chief?" The comment was followed by more mighty guffaws.

Marty looked up to see the big man standing at the table, shaking his boulder-like head with disgust. The guy clutched a Coke in his paw as if he were afraid it might try to wriggle free. He sorted through Marty's things with one, fat, hairy finger.

"You don't need any of this shit." He opened his jacket to reveal a large gun, hanging from a loose-fitting shoulder holster. "This is all you need to survive."

"You can't take a drink from a gun," Marty said.

"It's what you use to take one from somebody else, dumb fuck. You don't carry a fucking thing on your back, that's basic survival skills, no cucumbrances. Let some other dumb bastard drag the heavy shit around. Take what you want when you want it. That's the law according to Darwin, Smith, and Wesson."

The Chef set Marty's burrito and coke down in front of him. Marty glanced at the big guy, half expecting him to make a move on his meal. The big guy grinned, all yellow teeth and swollen gums.

"No thanks," the guy pulled out a chair and sat down. "I'm full."

Marty took a bite out of his burrito. It was hot, salty, and sticky with cheese. Incredibly delicious. He couldn't take a second bite fast enough.

"Makes you wonder why other Heeb food isn't this good, doesn't it?"

Marty washed down his mouthful of burrito with some Coke. It was very sweet, very cold, and absolutely wonderful. This was ranking as one of the best meals of Marty's life, despite the present company.

"You a cop?" Marty asked.

"Better than that," he reached into his breast pocket and dealt Marty his business card, a fresh, greasy fingerprint on the edge. Buck Weaver, licensed bounty hunter, skip tracer, and private investigator. "I just brought in Paco Pandito."

Marty shrugged, his mouth full.

"Only the meanest, nastiest, saltiest mother-fucker in the western United States," Buck said. "Carjacking, dope-dealing, coke-sniffing, cock-sucking bastard, that's who he is. Caught him at the outlet mall outside of Barstow. Can't resist discount clothing. That's his weakness. Pistol-whipped him as he came out of Tommy Hilfiger, then kicked him in the balls to keep him pleasant on the drive back. 'Course it's hard to be too unpleasant when you're riding in the fucking trunk."

Buck slurped on his coke. "I would've stayed in Barstow if I knew I was driving back for the goddamn Big One. At least I got my cash before it hit."

Marty nodded, wolfing down his Burrito, taking breaks between bites for drags on his Coke. The way Buck was studying him, Marty wondered if the guy was about to snatch the burrito out of his hands. It made him eat even faster.

"You got that sleazy, insincere look of a car salesman or a lawyer," Buck stated. "Am I right?"

"Network executive," Marty replied.

"What the fuck is that?"

"I make TV shows," Marty explained.

"You write them?"

"No."

"You produce them?"

"No."

"You direct them?"

"No."

Buck slammed his fist on the table, frustrated and not too happy about it. "Then how the fuck do you make them?"

Marty finished his burrito and sucked the last bit of cola from around the ice cubes as he thought about his answer. The fact is, the shows could get made without his involvement at all. He served no real creative function beyond making sure the network was getting the show it paid for. But no network executive in town let his role stop there, not if he wanted to get anywhere in this business. The key was to seem involved enough in the show to take credit for all its success, but remain distant enough to take none of the blame for its failure. That was the mark of a great network executive.

"I provide guidance to the writers, producers, and directors," Marty said. "I give very constructive notes."

"You call that a fucking job?" Buck snorted.

"It's a profession," Marty replied, defensive. Why was he arguing with this man?

"What good is it going to do you now?"

"About as much as yours."

"I got the fucking ability to survive out there," Buck said. "What the fuck you got? Notes? Give me one of your great fucking notes."

Marty looked him in the eye. The big, hulking, knuckle-dragging Neanderthal in a polyester suit and Treasure Island casino tie.

"It's encumbrance," Marty said, "not cucumbrance."

Buck leaned slowly forward. "What the fuck you say?"

"You said you don't want any cucumbrances," Marty sneered. "Sounds like you don't want to carry around any vegetables."

Buck yanked out his gun and put the barrel right against Marty's forehead. "One squeeze and you become a cucumbrance."

Marty froze. The sheer idiocy of the situation struck him more than the fear of death. He'd survived the earthquake, only to get killed because he stopped to eat a Kosher burrito and correct a sociopath's pronunciation. No one else in the place seemed to notice. They hadn't noticed the earthquake, why should they notice a murder?

Marty held Buck's fish-eyed gaze for a long moment. But instead of shooting, Buck broke into a smile and shoved the gun back into his holster.

"Get it? A fucking cucumbrance." Buck clapped Marty on the shoulder, two friendly cavemen sharing a fire. "You didn't think I was a funny guy, did you?"

Marty could still feel the imprint of the barrel against his forehead. He quickly got up and swept his stuff back into his pack. It was time to get the hell out of here. Why had he stopped in the first place?

"You're right, that was a great fucking note," Buck said, getting to his feet, blocking Marty's escape. "You got some balls."

One noticeably larger than the other, or so he'd been told, a condition that could explain his indecisiveness, undue caution, and unmotivated sperm.

"I just want to go home," Marty said.

"Which way you headed?"

"West."

Buck put his arm around Marty and dragged him into the street. "What do you know? So am I."

CHAPTER FOUR

The Lights Are Much Brighter There, You Can Forget All Your Troubles, Forget All Your Cares

12 :25 p.m. Tuesday
The streets were clogged with people now, hundreds of government workers, lawyers, jurors, marshals, judges, transients, parking lot attendants, and LA Times reporters. They milled around, trying to stay clear of the burning buses, the smoking cars, the fallen buildings, the wailing of the injured, the stink of the dead.

Buck pushed and shoved his way through them, clearing a path for himself and Marty up 1st Street as it rose over Bunker Hill. Marty realized there might be some advantages to having Buck along after all.

Marty had only traveled a mile or two since leaving the set, but it was a hard walk, making his way over ruined streets strewn with chunks of disgorged asphalt. Already his feet felt swollen, his knees were sore, and he was gasping for breath. If he kept deteriorating like this, Marty thought, he might need Buck to give him CPR in a couple more miles. He resolved at that moment to go back to the gym and use that membership, if the gym was still standing, or if it wasn't, just jog around the rubble three or four times each day.

As he ascended Bunker Hill, Marty clearly remembered the last two times he'd been downtown. The first was five years ago, when he and Beth came down to get a wedding license and meet with the family court judge who was going to marry them. The judge seemed to embody the full force of the law, as if personally schooled by John Houseman in the art of glowering intimidation. But when he performed their wedding, he seemed to be channeling Henny Youngman instead, apparently using their vows as a chance to try out a possible Vegas lounge act.

The second time was about a year ago, to talk his way out of serving on jury duty. All it took was an autographed photo of Jennifer Garner and a promise to read the clerk's spec screenplay when he finished it. Marty still hadn't gotten it and, judging by the damage to the County Courthouse, stomped under one of Mother Nature's enormous Doc Martens, he probably never would.

"Hey, did you piss yourself?" Buck glanced at Marty's pants.

"That's Evian," Marty replied between labored breaths.

"Yeah," Buck snorted. "I bet you shit Beluga caviar, too."

Abraham Lincoln's bronzed, decapitated head rolled past Marty as he paused at the corner of Hill and 1st and looked at the glimmering, downtown office towers a few blocks south. Buck was more interested in watching Honest Abe's head roll through the intersection than appreciating the view.

The only way you could really see the polished granite and tinted glass monoliths was from a distance, up close they were about as welcoming and creative as a retaining wall. They were each designed to make a grand architectural statement that could be absorbed in one glance from the freeway. Now they were all shedding glass like tears.

From where Marty stood on the crest of Bunker Hill, catching his breath, he could even see the future, or at least the building that stood in for it in a thousand bad TV shows and movies. The Bonaventure Hotel was five giant glass cylinders waiting to blast off a concrete launch pad into outer space. Today it looked like the launch finally happened, only the rockets had exploded before lift-off.

The studios would have to find the future somewhere else.

"Now that's what I call fucking ironic," Buck snorted. Following the course of Abe's wayward, bronzed noggin, Buck inadvertently spotted something interesting.

"What?" Marty asked.

"Look at that," Buck pointed a block south, where the old, brick Kawada Hotel still stood at the corner of 2nd and Hill, the sign for their Epicenter Café intact. "Isn't that fucking ironic?"

"Uh-huh," Marty continued on up the street, wondering for maybe the eighth time in five minutes why Buck wouldn't go away. But he told himself it couldn't hurt to have a big guy with a big gun at his side, especially considering the bad neighborhoods he'd soon be walking through.

"I appreciate ironic, witty stuff like that," Buck said. "Kind of goes against my hard-ass personality. Makes me so goddamn colorful you want to fuck me, doesn't it?"

Marty heard cries from the Department of Water and Power, a boxy building erected on a parking structure, the top level of which had been turned into a square lake, creating a moat around the edifice. The forty-year-old architectural conceit had turned into a trap now that the parking structure had pancaked onto itself and the contemporary drawbridge connecting the building to the street had fallen. The DWP workers were stranded in a collapsing building, but could rationalize their fate as the price of working in a bureaucratic fairy tale.

"I once saved a puppy dog," Buck added. "They were gonna kill the drooling little fur ball for protecting his home against an intruder. I couldn't live with the fucking injustice, with the idea of this poor, fluffy creature dying for doing the right thing, so I took a goddamn moral stand. The night before they were gonna give him the needle, I broke him out of the pound and let him live in my Mercury Montego."

Buck looked to Marty for congratulations and got incredulity instead.

"What kind of puppy?" Marty asked.

"What fucking difference does it make?"

"Was it a pit bull?"

"It was a pit bull puppy," Buck snapped. "They are just as fucking adorable as any other fucking puppy."

"And this intruder, what exactly was he doing?"

"Climbing over the fence into the dog's territory, that's what, after disturbing the animal's peace in a terrifying manner."

"He terrified a vicious pit bull," Marty said.

"The kid's baseball slammed into the dog house, scaring the

crap out of the dog, then the idiot kid climbed into the yard to get his ball. Okay? The point is, the dog doesn't know a fucking baseball from fucking gorilla and did what came naturally, defending himself and his goddamn master. So what I did was a fucking humanitarian act."

"He was your dog, wasn't he?" Marty asked. "And he mauled a child."

"You are missing the fucking point, asshole." Buck stabbed the air between them with his fat finger. "I got depth of character and thousands of great stories."

Marty was finally getting it. "You're pitching me a series, right? About you?"

"Why the hell not? You ever see a guy like me on TV?"

Only on Jerry Springer. "Call my secretary and make an appointment."

"We're having our appointment right now, dumbfuck" Buck said. "You got some other pressing engagement?"

The world had literally fallen down around them and Marty was expected to take a pitch. But he couldn't say this was the worst circumstances under which he'd been forced to listen to TV series ideas. His male fertility specialist was examining Marty's scrotum, feeling around his uneven balls, when he offered the observation: "Some incredible characters walk through these doors. You wouldn't believe the hilarious stories."

"Really?" Marty said, trying to act as if it was perfectly natural to be standing there, his pants around his ankles, a guy rolling his testicles in his hands, discussing series concepts.

"I got them all on index cards, they are absolute gold, funnier than 'Seinfeld.' You want to see them?"

Marty was afraid to say no, considering the guy literally had him by the balls. The situation wasn't all that much different today, but Marty's attitude certainly was. A year ago, his wife was sitting in the waiting room, and he could feel her yearning desperation through the walls. He needed the doctor happy. He needed his lopsided balls producing guided-missile sperm.

He didn't need Buck.

"Look around you," Marty told Buck. "We just survived the big one. Thousands of people are dead. The city is in ruins. Do you really think this is the best time to pitch a TV series to me?"

"Absolutely. We're bonding. When this is all over, we'll have a foundation to do some business together," Buck replied. "What's your name?"

"Martin Slack."

"All the detectives on TV are pussies, Marty. Do-gooders who only care about helping people and don't give a shit about getting paid. Everybody cares about getting paid, so that's bullshit. How the fuck they make the payments on their sports cars and buy all those expensive suits if they don't get paid? Tell me that."

Marty was about to tell him about the last detective show he worked on, just this morning in fact, when he came down the other side of Bunker Hill, saw the Harbor Freeway, and forgot everything he was going to say. Hundreds of cars were tangled together, charred and aflame, strewn over six lanes of up-ended roadway and fallen overpasses, stretching on for miles. If there was anybody screaming or crying under it all, the forlorn wail of agonized automobiles drowned them out.

Los Angeles was nothing but the intersection of vast freeways, and Marty knew they must all look like this—a line of ants squirted with lighter fluid, set aflame, then smacked a few times with a brick.

The death toll was unthinkable. And help would never come. It was caught dead in traffic.

Marty pulled the dust mask over his nose and mouth and pondered his options. He could climb the embankment and cross the carnage on the freeway, or he could walk underneath it, where the 110 passed over 1st Street. The overpass was still standing, but who knew how stable it was? How fast could he run twenty yards? How lucky did he feel?

Buck made his choice, he was already striding under the overpass, yelling back at Marty to hurry the fuck up. Marty knew Buck didn't give it any thought at all, he just moved forward with all the intellectual self-reflection of an amoeba.

Marty didn't think he could wade through the mess on the freeway, but it was suicide to go under an overpass that had already been weakened by two earthquakes in one morning. So that left only one choice. Blunder on like Buck. Only a hell of a lot faster.

"Shit," Marty muttered, than ran as fast as he could, using the ascent to give him some momentum into the overpass. He was half-way through the overpass when he tripped over a hunk of concrete.

Marty went sliding, as if trying to make first base. Lying flat on his stomach, nose to the asphalt, he heard the rumble and knew what was coming. Aftershock. He scrambled to his feet and started running again, knowing he was too late, knowing he'd be squished by tons of concrete in a second.

He ran screaming out from under the overpass, tripping again, rolling onto his back, turning in time to see a wave of fire sweeping across the top of the freeway, cars exploding like popcorn in its wake. The rumble he felt wasn't an aftershock, it was a chain-reaction explosion rolling up the 110.

The fire moved like water, washing over the freeway and then dissipating like it never existed at all, a blistering figment of Marty's over-worked imagination. But he knew it wasn't. Just one more unbelievable sight in a day already too full of them.

Marty got to his feet and spotted Buck, his back to him, pissing against the cyclone fence of the half-finished, $150 million Belmont High School. If the bounty hunter saw the fire, it hadn't made much of an impact on him, at least not one strong enough to ignore his bladder. He seemed much more interested in relieving himself on the most expensive high school in the world, its construction halted and abandoned mid-way through because somebody discovered it was built atop toxic waste. But at least the school was earthquake safe.

Buck zipped up his fly and turned to see Marty. "I got a few notes on your running. First, tie your fucking shoes."

Marty looked down at his feet. Both shoes were untied. His glasses slid off his nose and shattered on the ground.

"Second, you run like a pansy-ass fag," Buck said. "Are you a pansy-assed fag?"

"No," Marty said, tying his shoes. "I'm married."

"To a woman?"

"Yes, to a woman."

"Was she always a woman?"

Marty glared at him, saw Buck's gingivitis grin, and stomped on his glasses, grinding them into plastic crumbs.

"That's where I'm going," Marty said, "back home to her. Where are you going?"

"I'm going home, too."

They started walking again, side by side, down the nearly deserted street. Where was everybody? After a moment, Marty asked Buck: "Where's home?"

"Hollywood."

"You got anybody waiting for you?"

Buck shook his head no.

"So what's your hurry?"

Buck gave him a cold look. "Where the hell else would you go?"

Marty turned his gaze ahead, where 1st Street rose again, this time as an arched, concrete overpass that stretched across Glendale Boulevard. It seemed intact, with one car stalled at the crest, but Marty wasn't going to press his luck. He'd walk around the overpass and rejoin 1st Street on the other side of Glendale Boulevard.

"What's her name," Buck asked.

"Beth."

"What's she do?"

"She was an actress but she gave it up."

"Did I ever see her in anything?"

"No."

"How the fuck would you know?" Buck snapped. "You know every show I've ever seen? Give me some titles."

Marty listed a few by rote. "They Eat Their Own 2, Summer Wine, The Endless Spiral." Not the most illustrious resumé, Beth would be the first to agree. Her most lucrative gig was an antacid commercial that ran off and on for years.

"The Endless Spiral, was that the thing with Christopher Walken as the ghost assassin guy?"

"Yeah."

"Was she the girl Christopher Walken finger-fucked in the taxi?"

Yes.

"No," Marty replied. It was after sitting through that unbearable scene, Christopher Walken sitting right next to them in the screening, that Marty finally agreed to have a child, on the condition she'd give up acting for a while and become a stay-at-home Mom.

"I see a lot of bad fucking liars in my field," Buck said, "and you are the fucking worst. How could you let some guy finger-fuck your wife?"

"It was Christopher Walken and they were acting."

"That looked like a finger in her twat to me," Buck said.

"It was a stunt twat," Marty said. "Can we just drop it?"

Clearly Buck was enjoying himself too much to let it go, and he probably wouldn't have, if it weren't for the panic-stricken, Mexican man who ran up to them, babbling in Spanish. It was easy for Marty to just keep going and ignore him, but Buck stopped and answered the guy in what sounded remarkably like fluent Spanish. That stopped Marty for a moment, a moment he'd soon regret.

He understood a few of the words—Boy, Car, Trapped—and looked again at the overpass.

Marty saw now that the overpass wasn't intact at all, it was split apart at the crest, a Toyota teetering over the jagged edge, tangled in the splintered rebar. The windshield was shattered, a body splattered on the street directly below the car.

The driver should have worn a seat belt.

Buck shoved him. "This guy says there's a kid in that car up there, buckled in the seat, too fucking scared to move."

"I don't blame him," Marty said, starting to walk away. Buck grabbed him.

"The guy needs our help to get the kid out."

Marty shook his head. "Do I look like Charlton Heston to you?"

"What the fuck?"

"I'm not a hero." Marty turned away, and again Buck grabbed him.

"Maybe I'm not making myself fucking clear here. There's a kid alone in that car up there. He's trapped."

"So are a thousand other kids in this city. Am I supposed to save each one of them?"

Buck let go of Marty and looked him right in the eye. "You are going to save this one."

"No," Marty said. "I'm going home."

He adjusted his gym bag on his shoulders, turned his back to Buck, and headed west. Molly was enough. More than anyone had a right to ask of him. He'd done his part, he didn't have to do any more. His only obligation was to get home to his wife.

Marty heard the click. The Dirty Harry click. The sound was almost subliminal. He knew what it was from a lifetime of vicarious experience. Although nobody had ever pointed a gun at him and cocked the trigger before, he'd heard it on TV so many times, he knew the sound instinctively.

"Take one more step asshole and I'll shoot you," Buck said behind him.

He stopped and looked over his shoulder. Yep, Buck was aiming a gun at him for the second time today. Behind Buck, the Mexican guy was waving his hands, jabbering in a desperate torrent of unintelligible Spanish, clearly afraid he'd been terribly misunderstood.

Marty spoke clearly and slowly.

"I've been through this already, Buck. That's why my backpack was on fire. That's how close I came to dying. You want to be a hero? Go for it. I hope you survive, but I can't risk it again. I have to make it home, for my wife. That is my moral obligation. Okay?"

But Marty didn't get anything back from Buck and he'd be damned if he was going to argue about it. So Marty just started walking.

And Buck shot him.

Marty heard the unbelievably loud gunshot the same instant he felt the scorching punch in his shoulder, spinning him around and knocking him off his feet.

His shoulder was burning. He touched the bloody tear in his jacket and, his ears still ringing, stared back at Buck incredulously. "You shot me?"

"I grazed you," Buck said. "Don't be a pussy."

Marty's fury overwhelmed his pain. "You don't have any one, it doesn't matter if you get killed trying to save everybody. There's no one waiting for you, no one depending on you."

"That kid is," Buck said. "Look around you, asshole. You're alive. You have two good arms and two good legs. Your fucking obligation is to help everyone you see, whether you want to or not. So, you got a choice. You can die a hero trying to save that kid or you can die a coward right now. You decide."

Marty glanced up at the car, creaking in the breeze, then at the bloody lump on the pavement. In a few minutes, if he gave in, that could be him. Only with a car and maybe the entire overpass on him. Even the homeless were smart enough to flee from the fractured overpass, leaving behind their flea-ridden mattresses, piles of soiled blankets, and plastic bags of garbage.

The crumbling overpass, the swaying car, they were death traps. Attempting this rescue, without the necessary equipment or any experience, was suicide.

It was like all those stories he'd read in the LA Times, the ones about people who drowned trying to save someone who fell through ice or got sucked under the sea by a riptide. Instead of one unfortunate person dying, three or four would-be rescuers inevitably sacrificed their lives as well.

Those stories, buried in the bottom corner of the back pages, always struck Marty as sad, tragic, and stupid. He liked to think that if he were in one of those situations he'd know to choose survival over unthinking heroism, no matter how wrenching that decision would be.

But he'd never been in one of those situations.

He also never had to make a decision at gunpoint before.

It changed things.

"Put the gun away." Marty said.

Buck kept it on him.

"Put the fucking gun away," Marty yelled. "I can't think with that pointed at me."

"There's nothing to think about."

"Do you know how to get the kid out without knocking the car over the edge? Do you, you fucking psychopath?" Marty stared at him, at the blank look on his face. "I didn't think so."

Buck holstered his gun. "You got some rope in your pack. We'll lower you down."

"First of all, that rope is for tying up a roll of electric cables, it's not strong enough to hold a man," Marty said. "Secondly, why am I the guy?"

"Because you're the lightest of the three of us," Buck said. "And even if you weren't, you've been shot in the arm."

"You said I was grazed."

"Stop being a pussy," Buck said.

Marty looked at the teetering car again, then down at the pavement, and the body splattered on it. His eyes drifted from the body to the pile of filthy blankets and he remembered something he saw on Cinemax late one night, one of those soft-core women-in-prison movies. The busty, sexually-adventurous convicts escaped using bed-sheets. It wasn't a very secure prison, the guards weren't too bright, but the girls were pretty resourceful and the principle was sound.

Marty clutched his bloody shoulder and got up. "I got an idea. You're going to have to find a few more people to help."

1:30 p.m. Tuesday
The smell from the urine-starched blankets tied around his chest and wrapped under his shoulders was overpowering. If the drop didn't kill Marty, the odor would.

The bum's blankets were tied together end-to-end and securely wound with Marty's rope. The apparatus trailed behind him a few feet to Buck, Enrique, and half-a-dozen other survivors who held the other end as if preparing for a game of tug-of-war.

Marty stood on the edge of the precipice, beside the Toyota, gathering his courage. The ticks, fleas, and lice were probably smart enough to abandon the blankets now. No sense taking a fall with this fool, a guy who mistook *Caged Party Bimbos* for an instructional video on urban rescues.

"We're ready," Buck yelled.

"I'm not," Marty muttered, pulling his leather work gloves tight over his hands.

The car was hanging by just one rear wheel, held in place by just a few pieces of twisted rebar. He couldn't see the kid, the car was tipped too far forward, but he could hear him whining in terror.

Marty had no idea what he was going to do, except not look down. He turned to the men holding the rope, strangers he didn't know an hour ago and still didn't know right now. He was entrusting them, and a make-shift rope made of a dozen soiled blankets, with his life.

"You sure you can hold me?" Marty asked.

"Two more seconds and I'll push you," Buck said. "Stop stalling. That car isn't going to hold much longer."

Marty took a deep breath and moved right up to the edge. It was a long drop. Chances of survival if he fell were zero.

"Shit," he whispered, sitting down.

He grabbed two pieces of rebar and slid slowly over the edge, bits of concrete shaking loose, falling into space and shattering on the street below.

Shit. Shit. Shit.

Marty slid a bit further, his legs dangling over the side. Soon there would be nothing for him to hold on to at all.

"Do you have me?" he yelled.

"Hurry the fuck up," Buck grunted.

Marty let go of the rebar and fell, screaming. The blanket dug into Marty's armpits, jerking his shoulders up against his neck. But it held, stopping his fall, but jerking the cell phone out of his pocket. He dangled, spinning beside the car, making the mistake of looking down just as his cell phone shattered on the pavement.

Oh God.

Not only was he going to die, now he couldn't call anyone to tell them about it.

He reached out and touched the car to stop his spin, and that's when he saw the kid, buckled into the front seat, eyes wide with horror, hands out in front of him, flat against the dashboard. The kid was black, maybe six or seven years old. He was staring at Marty like he was a big, vicious spider hanging outside the window.

"Stay calm," Marty said, "Don't move."

As if the kid was going anywhere. What a dumb thing to say. But Marty couldn't think of anything else. He wasn't even sure how to get the kid out of there without tipping the car over. Opening the door was probably too risky. It could shift things too suddenly.

"What's your name?"

"Franklin!" It came out as a scream.

"Okay, Franklin, here's what we're going to do. You're going to roll down the window."

The kid looked at him and shook his head, his teeth chattering in fright. No fucking way, not for this guy.

"You have to," Marty said, his voice cracking with fear. If he was counting on winning the kid over with his own courage, he could forget about it.

The kid just kept shaking his head. "No!"

"Listen, kid, I know how stupid and scared I look. Some jerk in a bunch of dirty blankets. You think you'd rather take your chances in the car." From the expression on Franklin's face, Marty knew he read the kid right. "But Franklin, the truth is, the car is going to fall and you will die. I may get you killed, too, but at least you will have tried to save yourself."

The kid looked at him, then looked forward, out the broken windshield at the ground below. Marty knew what he was thinking about. He was thinking about it, too.

"What would he want you to do?" Marty asked.

The blanket slipped a bit, shaking free more chunks of concrete. Marty inadvertently screamed again, grabbing at the air.

"Stop fucking around!" Buck yelled from above.

Something in Buck's voice, perhaps the violence and anger,

must have made a difference, because Franklin slowly rolled down the window. The car swayed and creaked as he slightly shifted his weight. Marty gently reached into the open window and held the door to steady himself. He could see that Franklin had wet his pants. Marty didn't blame him.

"Okay, here's what we're going to do. You're going to unbuckle yourself, grab hold of my arm, and I'm going to slowly pull you out."

Franklin stared at him. "I can't."

"You have to, Franklin." Marty said. "I won't drop you. I promise." He hoped it was a promise he could keep. His mind immediately, uncontrollably flashed to that horrific, opening scene in *Cliffhanger.*

Franklin must have seen the doubt skirt across Marty's eyes. "I want to wait for the firemen."

They were losing valuable seconds. And the longer Marty dangled, the more terrified Marty was becoming. What little resolve he had was fading fast and so was the strength of the men holding him. Marty imagined what the audience was seeing and he wasn't, the loose knots slowly becoming unfurled, the blanket ripping on the sharp edge of concrete. And they would all be screaming, why doesn't that dumb fucking idiot do something?

"Franklin, there are no firemen. There will never be any firemen. I am it. Now get out of the goddamn car."

The kid started crying again, but he unbuckled his belt. Franklin immediately fell forward against the dash, the car teetering suddenly with the shift in weight. Marty reached in, grabbed the back of Franklin's shirt with both hands, and yanked with all his strength just as the Toyota pitched forward, falling free.

Franklin dangled from Marty's hands, his shirt riding up his body, his legs kicking in open space, as the car flipped end-over-end and smacked into the ground below. Marty and the kid were both screaming now, spinning in the air, hanging in terror.

God, the kid was heavy. Marty had never held anything so heavy, it felt like the kid was tearing his arms from his sockets, ripping tendons, shredding muscles. He couldn't possibly hold him another second.

The kid grabbed Marty and hugged him tightly, his face pressed against Marty's legs, muffling his cries. But Marty screamed loud and hard, from the bottom of his lungs, enough for both of them.

Buck and Enrique pulled them up onto the overpass and dragged them a few feet from the edge before letting go. The kid broke free of Marty the second they were safe and ran, sobbing. Enrique chased after him, caught him, and pulled him into a hug.

Marty sat up, pulling the piss-soaked blankets off as fast as he could. Buck offered him his hand. Marty swatted it away.

"Get away from me," Marty said, shakily getting to his feet. He was shivering all over. Buck reached out to him again and Marty punched him in the face.

It wasn't much of a punch, not much more than a slap, really. His fist was shaking too much to have any power behind it. But it was the first time Marty had swung at anyone since third grade. His pugilistic skills hadn't improved any since then.

Marty was as surprised by the punch as Buck was, but he didn't regret it. Marty had never been so angry or so scared.

Buck could easily have flattened Marty with a return blow. Instead, the big man just grinned.

"Who taught you how to fight? The same clown who showed you how to run?" Buck said. "That's got to change if you're gonna pull off this hero shit."

"I don't want to be a hero," Marty screamed at him. "I'd like to live."

"Take it easy. Now that you've done it, it will be easier next time."

"I'm going home," Marty found his back pack and put it on. "I'm not stopping for anybody, do you understand me?"

Buck walked towards him. "We'll see what happens."

Marty pointed at Buck and backed away. "Stay the hell away from me, you crazy, psycho, son-of-a-bitch."

"We're going the same way."

"I'm going alone," Marty said. "I don't want to see you ever again."

Buck looked at Marty, truly dumbfounded. "What are you so pissed off for?"

Marty couldn't believe what he was hearing. What was there the guy didn't get?

"You shot me," Marty yelled. "You wrapped me in piss blankets and dangled me off the edge of a collapsed overpass!"

"That part was your idea. And what the fuck difference does it make now? You saved the kid's life."

Yes, he did.

Marty turned and looked at Franklin, still crying, still hugging Enrique, a complete stranger. The nightmare was over. Thanks to Marty Slack.

He'd actually plucked a frightened child from a car teetering on the brink of a three-story drop.

Holy shit.

Maybe there was a little Charlton Heston in him after all.

Marty felt a proud smile starting on his face and quickly suppressed it, reminding himself that he was angry. Furious. Outraged.

He shot you. He forced you into this at gunpoint. You could have been killed! The only reason you're still alive is dumb luck. How much more of that do you think you have left?

The scowl returned. He turned back to confront Buck.

"I could just as easily have ended up dead, because you put a gun to my head and made me do that stupid, suicidal stunt," Marty said. "You are a homicidal Neanderthal psycho. I don't want you near me, understand? Go away. Get somebody else killed."

Marty turned around and marched off, passing Enrique and Franklin without looking at them. He didn't want to be drawn in any deeper into the kid's problems, or Enrique's for that matter. All he wanted to do was go home, put as many miles between himself and all of this as he could.

"Stop or I'll shoot," Buck said.

He gave Buck the finger without looking back and kept right on walking.

CHAPTER FIVE
Going Nowhere Fast

2:20 p.m. Tuesday

Marty marched across Glendale Avenue, heading west, staying clear of the overpass on his left.

It was already mid-afternoon and he'd only covered three or four miles since he started. But Marty felt like he'd already walked a hundred. Every joint in his body throbbed in pain. At this rate, it would take him days to get home.

He glanced to his right. He was passing a stark, white, windowless building that looked like a mausoleum. It might as well have been. A sign near the flat roof read "Bob Baker's Marionette Theatre," which was now showing a program called "It's a Musical World."

Marty had never heard of the place, and wondered who bothered coming to this godforsaken spot to see such rudimentary entertainment. What kid would chose to see a puppet on strings over his PlayStation, the Internet, or a digital-effects blockbuster on DVD? Seeing a show at the marionette theatre made as much sense to Marty as gathering in a cave to watch Grog scratch stick figures on the stone.

He was so caught up in distracting himself with a pointless rumination on the irrelevance of puppetry in a modern world that he didn't see the homeless man waving the rusty steak knife until they were face-to-face.

It looked like someone had used the bearded bum's scabby face to clean a couple hundred very dirty dishes. And he smelled just like Marty. A walking urinal.

"You stole my stuff," the man hissed through broken, rotting teeth. "I saw you."

So now Marty knew why they smelled alike. Those piss-soaked blankets belonged to this Brillo-faced guy.

"I didn't steal your blankets—" Marty started to say.

"I saw you," the bum interrupted. "Motherfucker."

"I just borrowed them to rescue the kid. You saw me rescue the kid, right?"

"Give me my stuff," the man repeated. "I want my stuff."

"I don't have it," Marty replied. "It's on the overpass. You're welcome to it. Thanks for the loan."

"Motherfucker," The bum thrust the knife at Marty, nearly stabbing him with it. Marty jerked back defensively.

"Hey, I'm sorry about borrowing your stuff without asking, but it's all there, right on the overpass," Marty said. "I had to use them to save the kid. If you saw me take the blankets, you must have seen that, too."

The bum studied Marty with the goopy, glassy eyes of a hound. "Give me your stuff."

"Your blankets are up there. Just go get them."

"Give me your stuff." The bum motioned to the gym bag. "I want your stuff."

"No."

"Motherfucker!" The bum poked the air between them with the knife. "Give me your stuff or I'll stick you."

Marty knew he would, too. But there was no way he was giving up his survival kit. Certainly not in exchange for a pile of piss-drenched rags he never wanted to begin with. No, he was not giving his pack up.

"You want it?" Marty asked, slipping it off his shoulders. "Fine, you can have it. Motherfucker."

And with that, Marty lunged at him, holding the gym bag out directly in front of him. Marty pushed himself right into the point of bum's knife, which sunk harmlessly into the bag.

The surprised bum staggered back and, just as he realized he'd lost his weapon, there was a loud crack and he spun around, shoved aside by some invisible linebacker.

It took a moment for Marty to figure out what happened, to make sense of the sound, the bum on the ground, the blood pooling underneath him.

He'd been shot.

Marty whirled around to see Buck marching up, holding the gun casually at his side, a cocky grimace on his face. "Never fear, the professional is here."

"What the hell is the matter with you?" Marty immediately dropped his gym bag and knelt beside the bum, who was still alive, semi-conscious, groaning in pain. The wound was in his shoulder.

"I just saved your life," Buck said, "you inconsiderate fuck."

"I was handling it!" Marty tore open the man's blood-soaked shirt, recoiling at the smell and the flea-bitten skin.

"You couldn't handle your prick to piss." Buck peered down at his victim.

Marty gently turned the man over and saw the exit wound. The bullet had passed right through him. That was a good thing, wasn't it? He had no idea. Shit!

"You can't just go around shooting people!" Marty yelled at him.

"I can shoot whoever I want whenever I want," Buck replied casually. "I'm a licensed bounty hunter. Besides, this was self-defense."

"He wasn't threatening you," Marty snapped. "Get me the first aid kit in my bag."

"I was talking about your self defense, asshole," Buck picked up the bag. "Did he or did he not threaten you with a knife?"

"I disarmed him!"

"Your method of disarming an individual is almost as impressive as your method of delivering a punch," snorted Buck, dropping the bag dismissively, the knife still impaled in it, at Marty's feet. "You're owed a refund on your manhood."

Marty unzipped the bag, tore open the plastic first aid kit, and flipped frantically through the ridiculously small brochure. Bee stings, blisters, broken arms—where the hell was the chapter on bullet wounds?

Buck sighed wearily. "What the fuck are you looking for?"

"Instructions!" Marty retorted. "How do I stop the bleeding?"

"Like this, dumb fuck." Buck yanked the bum up into a sitting position, grabbed some gauze in each fist from the first aid kit, and applied pressure to both wounds. "Where have you been living?"

Marty looked at the two of them—the deranged, bleeding bum and the homicidal maniac who shot him—and stood up slowly on shaky knees.

"In another world," Marty said, "and I'm anxious to get back."

He snatched up his gym bag by one of the straps, plucked the steak knife out of it, and tossed it as far as he could. "You can keep the medical kit. You're going to need it."

"Where are you going?"

"Home. Haven't you been listening?" Marty pulled a fresh dust mask out of his pack, zipped it up, and looped the straps over his shoulders. "You're staying here and taking care of this man until help arrives."

"Like hell I am."

"Oh, you'll do it, Buck. Because when this is all over, I'm going to tell the police what happened here today, that you shot him in cold blood. So, for your sake, you better hope he doesn't bleed to death."

Buck shook his head. "Twenty, thirty thousand people probably died today. You really think anyone is going to care what happened to some filthy homeless guy?"

"We're all filthy homeless guys now, Buck," Marty pulled the dust mask on and adjusted it over his nose and mouth. "Don't forget to give him back his blankets. He really wants them back."

And with that, Marty headed off once again. Reeking of sweat, cordite, gasoline, and another man's piss. Feeling the pain of a dozen scrapes, countless bruises, and one passing bullet. Carrying the fresh memories of one dead woman, one terrified boy, and one homeless man wielding a rusty steak knife.

A lifetime of horrible experiences crammed into one morning, and he still wasn't out of this yet. It didn't seem possible. It certainly wasn't fair.

He didn't know how much more of this he could take. The earthquake and the extreme damage it caused still seemed distant, unreal, even though he'd walked through it. But all of this, the smells and pains he carried with him, were far too personal and

50

almost too ugly to face. He didn't do a thing for Molly, leaving her trapped to die in a fireball. At least he made up for that failure with Franklin.

He'd done his big, daring, heroic act. He was sitting out the rest of this catastrophe.

All Marty wanted to do was clear his head, to forget the suffering he had witnessed and the suffering he had caused, to make his mind a blank until he got to his doorstep.

Failing that, he'd settle for just an hour of peace, a chance to regroup, maybe find the strength that was cowering in some dark corner of his soul and coax it to come out.

All of his misfortune, all of the danger he'd been in, could be traced to his inability to abide by his own rules. That was going to change, starting now.

Marty rejoined 1st Street, which became Beverly Boulevard as it rose up hill on the other side of the overpass. To his left, a block-long mural had been painted on the retaining wall that held together the soil of the old Belmont High School's football field, where hundreds of frightened kids were now gathered outside.

He was beginning at the end of a mural charting the life of man. It started in the future, showing a smiling, multi-ethnic group of Los Angelenos walking hand-in-hand into a Jetsons' future of streamlined buildings and flying cars. And as Marty moved west, the mural took him back in time, past Indian camps and buffalo, past cavemen and saber-toothed tigers, right back to single-cell organisms floating blissfully ignorant in puddles of muck and the cosmic explosion that started it all.

B eth straddled him, her hands flat against his chest, her face crinkled with concentration, working steadily towards her climax. He liked watching her like this, her skin flushed and damp, her eyes lids heavy, her mouth slightly parted, her small breasts swaying with the urgent motion.

And when she finally got there, there was a sharp intake of breath, her jaw dropped, and she ground even more hurriedly against him, chasing the moment, not letting it escape until the last possible second, her entire body tensed up, her nipples drawn into hard points.

He grabbed her then, giving up to it, because for him it wasn't a pursuit, but a losing battle, a fight against an ever strengthening force that he always knew would, and he desperately wanted, to overpower him.

Beth collapsed on his chest, breathing heavily, fresh perspiration on her back. Max thumped his tail excitedly on the hardwood floor, almost like an audience stamping their feet with applause. The dog loved it when they made love. He lay there, his head on a pile of scripts, watching them like an approving teacher. Marty hated having the dog in the room, he found it distracting. More than once the damn dog stuck his nose in the wrong place at the wrong time.

"We can't do this forever," she said huskily.

"Why not?" he whispered back, kissing her head.

"Because it's two o'clock in the afternoon on a Thursday. We should be working."

"I am," he said. "The deeper I explore our relationship, the deeper I understand the characters I write."

"That's bullshit," she gave him a playful squeeze.

"Of course it is," he smiled back. "This is better than work. This is what people wish they were doing when they're working."

Beth slid off him and lay on her side, facing him, propping her head up with one hand. Her freckles seemed even darker afterwards, and she had that delicious smell of sex and so did he. He loved this moment best of all.

"It's great, and I love it, too. But we have to be practical. Neither one of us is making any money." She ran a finger around his belly button, traced the line of hair up to his chest. "If it weren't for the residuals from my Captain Crunch commercial, we wouldn't have made the rent this month."

Why did she have to talk about this now? Why did they even have to talk about it at all? The rent was paid, that month was behind them. They'd deal with the next month when it happened.

"Something will come up," Marty said. "You'll get a series or a big movie, I'll sell one of my scripts. We'll make it."

She kissed him, hard and desperate, on the lips then leaned over him thoughtfully. "I love you, and I believe in you, but we have to be honest."

"Okay."

"You haven't finished any of your scripts," she said, almost guiltily.

"I know how to tell a good story," Marty sat up, turning his back to her. "I just have a little trouble writing them. I'll crack it."

She put her arms around him and pressed herself against his back. "I know, but until then, maybe you should think about doing something else."

"I'm a writer."

"But you can make $75 a script, reading for the studios," she said. "Maybe, for a while, you could write less and read more."

For months, he'd supplemented their income reading scripts and writing reports for executives too busy to read the stacks of submissions themselves. Reading that shit only made him more frustrated at his inability to finish a script of his own. He knew he could write better than these jerks. What scared him was that even if he managed to finish a script, some other frustrated writer, another "freelance reader," would be the one passing judgment on him. And he knew from personal experience just how petty and vindictive they could be.

"You're good at it," she said.

"At reading," he said. "I'm good at reading someone else's script. I can't write one, but I do a hell of a good job reading them. Wow. Now that's a remarkable talent."

"But you know how to make the scripts better, I've read your reports," she said. "You could turn a lousy script into a great movie."

"Someone else's script."

"It's a real talent, Marty. Not a lot of people can do that."

"That's all most people in this town do, tell other people how good or bad their scripts are because they can't write themselves."

"All I'm saying is that maybe you ought to try it full time for a while, until you crack whatever it is mentally that you have to crack."

"You don't think I can do it," Marty said, playing with his wedding ring. After nearly a year, he still wasn't used to it. "You don't think I can write."

"I think we need to make some money. I think maybe if we don't have to worry as much about making the rent, it will free you up to be more creative. You won't feel as much pressure."

That made some sense; he couldn't argue with that. He was very aware that she was the bread-winner, that she was supporting his long afternoons staring at an empty computer screen. It did choke him up creatively. The wind choked him up creatively. A book out of alphabetical order on the shelf choked him up creatively. It seemed everything did.

The truth was, there had been an offer. At one of the networks. An entry-level development position, reading scripts and books all day. He never told her about it because he knew she'd want him to take it.

"I love you, Marty. And I want you to be happy, to pursue whatever dreams you have." She turned his head toward her and gave him a kiss. "I'm just saying it's an option, that's all."

He nodded.

Beth kissed him again, got up and padded naked to the kitchen down the hall. God, he loved watching her walk naked, the casualness of it. How did he ever seduce her? How did he ever get her to fall in love with him?

The low rumble seemed to come hurtling towards them from a great distance yet arrived in an instant, unexpected and yet familiar. The whole house seemed to shiver, and then everything stopped, except for Beth's shrieks. She ran into the bedroom, dove onto the bed, and crawled up Marty, clutching him harder than she ever had before.

"What was that?" she cried, her whole body shaking.

"Just an earthquake."

"What do you mean, 'just an earthquake,'" she said. "Holy shit."

"It's nothing." Even the dog seemed undisturbed, yawning and stretching out across Marty's underwear and socks.

"Marty, the whole house shook, the ground was moving. It wasn't nothing."

"It's just an earthquake," he said, "3.4, tops."

"The ground moved, Marty. Shit. The ground moved." She started to cry, deep, terrified sobs, burying her face in his chest like a frightened child. For a moment, he was confused; he couldn't understand why a little shake had frightened her so much.

And then it dawned on him and he was ashamed of himself for not realizing it immediately. What kind of husband was he?

This was her first time. She'd never experienced an earthquake before.

How could he have been so dismissive? So unfeeling? He held her tightly, guiltily, kissing her, stroking her hair, over-doing it. "It's okay. It's going to be fine; it was just a small one. It's perfectly normal."

"The ground moved," she sniffled. "It's not supposed to."

"I know."

Beth was born and raised in Washington State, moving to California for UCLA, for Hollywood. She wasn't born here, growing up with the regular rumblings, under the ever-present threat of the inevitable, mythical, horrible Big One.

That was one concept he certainly wasn't going to share with her now.

"We can't live somewhere where the ground moves," she said. "We have to go, we have to get out of here. Someplace where the ground is . . . is . . . grounded."

"We can't afford to go any where right now," he said softly.

"As soon as we have the money, we'll go," she sniffled, lifted her head, and looked him in the eye. "You promise?"

"I'll get a reader job tomorrow." He kissed her and pulled her back down to him, knowing she'd forget about it in a day or so.

"The ground isn't supposed to move," she said again.

There had been more earthquakes since then, but like most people who lived for a while in LA, she got used to it. Even joked about it, in that blasé way Californians do, as he knew she would. But she wasn't fooling him. She never could completely hide the fear in her eyes. Marty wondered what her eyes looked like now and quickened his pace.

It had been a long time since he told Beth that he loved her. Oh sure, he'd said it, in that rote, "good-morning, how are you?" kind of way. But he didn't say it with feeling, not so she understood he needed her more than air. He knew he'd been withholding it and he didn't know why. And now, more than ever before, it was important to him that she knew that yes, he loved her.

Above him, an enormous flock of birds flew towards the sea, the world for them unshaken, safe. The air would never fail them, would never fall out from under their wings.

The ground isn't supposed to move. Everyone knew that. It was arrogance, and more than a little stupidity, to stay in a place where it did.

But what was Hollywood without arrogance and stupidity? You couldn't manufacture dreams if you weren't willing to live in one yourself.

Welcome to the flipside of the dream, asshole.

Now that Buck was gone, that little voice was back; not that they were all that much different. At least this one didn't have a gun.

You promised her you'd leave and you didn't. Just another broken promise in a pile of 'em, isn't that right, Marty?

Beth didn't really want to leave LA any more than he did. Their careers were here. And the more time that passed between quakes, the more abstract the threat became.

It wasn't abstract any more.

Home. He had to get home. But at the rate he was going, it would take him a week. It was already half-past three, and he was only four miles west of downtown. The Cahuenga Pass was about five miles northwest. He had to make better time or he wouldn't get to the valley by dark—and he certainly didn't want to be here when the sun went down.

His shoulder throbbed, his shirt sticking to his gunshot wound, becoming part of the scab. Marty could feel blisters rising on his heels. His entire body was drenched with sweat, making him stink even more, which he didn't think was possible without decomposing. He could only imagine what the smell was like without the protection of a dust mask.

He walked briskly up Beverly Boulevard, which no one would ever confuse for the western end that ran through the center of Beverly Hills. While the other end was paved with upscale boutiques, fancy restaurants, and pricey antique stores, this stretch catered to an entirely different clientele. Emilio's Discount. Pepe Ranchero. Mercado Latino. Catalina Carniceria. Not merchants that usually came to Marty's mind when someone mentioned Beverly Boulevard.

Marty glanced down the residential avenues that branched off the boulevard. The streets were lined with classic Victorian, Craftsman, English Tudor, and Spanish colonial houses with broad front yards, that would fetch upwards of $2 million each if they were in Beverly Hills, Hancock Park, or Pasadena. But these streets were ceded long ago to the tide of immigrants from Mexico, South America, and Asia who didn't have the means to maintain the properties in their original style and grace.

Long before the earthquake, decades of neglect, economic

hardship, and destructive improvements had taken their toll on the homes. Whatever architectural charms they once had were lost to iron-barred windows and cut-rate remodeling, cyclone fencing and junked cars parked on dead lawns. The once elegant porches were cluttered with old couches and Pontiac bucket seats, or closed in with chicken wire, transformed into open-air storage units.

Marty's Calabasas neighborhood would never end up like this. It was against the rules of his gated community. No additions or remodels were permitted without the approval of the architectural committee, which never approved anything. Flowers planted without the consent of the landscaping committee were immediately yanked out of the dirt. Cars not garaged at night were ticketed. Basketball hoops, motor homes, and boats were forbidden.

That was how you maintained property values. Put a wall around it and appoint committees.

But in this neighborhood, just a few miles west of downtown, it was hard, except in extreme cases, for Marty to discern what was earthquake damage to these homes and what was just lingering wounds.

Whatever their state of decay or damage, the houses now shared one thing in common. They were all empty. Entire families had fled their homes, dragging their TV sets and stereos, mattresses and clothes, iceboxes and recliners out onto the streets, setting up encampments in their front yards. They built impromptu shelters, stringing blankets, garbage bags, and tablecloths from the roofs of their cars to the tops of their cyclone fences, covering the sidewalks underneath with bedding.

Marty averted his gaze, afraid it would be met by one of the sad eyes in those shabby shelters, and he definitely didn't want to be drawn into anything there.

People were already mobbing the handful of small, earthquake-ravaged "Mercados" and "Supermercados" along the boulevard, picking through the rubble, searching aisles strewn with spilled and splattered merchandise for any surviving canned foods and bottled water.

As he passed the stores, he was stunned to see that the people, despite their desperation and fear, were still dutifully lining up at the registers to pay for what they found, fought over, and wrestled out of their neighbors' hands.

Marty didn't share their desperation, he still had enough food and water in his pack to make it home, where he and Beth had plenty of supplies stashed.

For a brief and satisfying moment, Marty once again felt like he'd conquered the quake with his cool head and superb preparation. The only itsy bitsy problem was the walk home. But in a few hours, that would be behind him and he'd be firmly in charge of the situation.

The important thing now was to learn from his recent mistakes and stick to his plan. Think only of getting home as quickly as possible. Think only about Beth and how much more she needed him than anyone else along the way.

Just ahead, beyond a curve in the boulevard, Marty could see a column of dark smoke. As he approached, he saw a fissure in the asphalt, a geyser of fire shooting out of it, flames lashing the buildings on either side of the street. All that was left of one blazing structure was its quirky, retro sign—a smiling cartoon character in a tuxedo, waving a chastising finger at a cockroach, distracting the insect from the mallet hidden behind his back.

The character seemed so familiar. He was trying to place the image when a dead bird smacked into the street at his feet. Marty looked up and saw two more birds plunging right at him.

He jumped aside, but it was futile. It was raining dead birds. The entire flock that had flown over his head moments ago were falling out of the sky all around him. They hit his body like baseballs, pummeling him to the ground.

And then he knew where he'd seen that cartoon character with the mallet. On the side of an exterminator's truck.

The birds were dying because they'd flown into a cloud of poison gas, the same one that was over his head right now.

CHAPTER SIX
A King Without His Throne

3:50 p.m. Tuesday
Marty scrambled to his feet and fled down the nearest side street, screaming "poison gas" as loud as he could.

But no one was listening to him.

For one thing, his words were muffled by his dust mask. For another, everyone was too busy evading the hailstorm of dead birds. The high-velocity, feathered bombs were pelting people off their feet, thunking into parked cars and collapsing make-shift shelters on impact. Compared to that, a lunatic running down the street yelling something unintelligible was easily ignored.

Marty ran in a panic, stumbling and tumbling over the debris in the street, stealing looks over his shoulder at the brown, roiling cloud of toxic smoke. He ran as if the dark cloud was alive and in pursuit, tendrils of insecticide reaching for him, hungry for his flesh. He ran until he couldn't anymore, until his stomach cramped up and each breath felt like a sword being shoved down his throat.

He pulled his dust mask down and looked back, relieved to see the noxious cloud was no longer above him but moving eastward, pushed by a gentle breeze. But Marty's sense of relief was obliterated by a body-buckling cramp and the sudden terror that he might lose control of his bowels.

And that possibility, that Marty might crap all over himself, right there in middle of the street, was more frightening to him than the toxic cloud ever was.

He didn't worry about whether he'd already been poisoned and this was just the beginning of a gruesome death. He didn't wonder if the horrible cramps were from the pesticide or his Authentic Kosher Mexican Burrito. The only thing Marty Slack was thinking about was finding a working toilet in the next sixty seconds, because that's how long his biological stopwatch told him he had until his sphincters burst open.

One of his worst nightmares, far more frightening than the Big One hitting, was the fear of losing control of his bowels without a toilet nearby. This nightmare was topped only by the fear of the big one hitting while he was on the toilet.

Even under normal circumstances, the idea of someone seeing him on a toilet, having a regular bowel movement, made Marty dizzy with terror. Even in his own home he locked the door whenever he used the bathroom—he couldn't face the possibility of Beth walking in on him.

Marty had already decided, moments after his decision to walk home from downtown, that he wouldn't take a dump for the next few days. He was determined to be constipated for the duration of the crisis or until he could find a porto-potty with a strong interior latch.

So much for his resolve.

Like every other promise Marty had made himself that day, this one would be broken, and within the next few seconds. His body was rebelling, his intestines twisting into braids. He had to do something.

Marty couldn't ask somebody if he could use their toilet because even if they said it was okay, he couldn't risk going into a house that might collapse on him. What he really needed was a hiding place.

He had ten seconds to find one.

Why hide? Drop your pants and get it over with, right here in the street, or on that lawn over there. Who's going to care? The city is in ruins. There are people bleeding and vomiting and dying all over the place; do you think anyone is going to give a damn about some guy taking a shit?

Marty couldn't do it. He *wouldn't* do it. There had to be someplace to hide.

Then he saw the court-yard apartment building on the corner, and the big, ragged hedge that ran alongside one wall. There was no one near it.

Clutching himself, Marty hobbled quickly to the hedge and dived into it, scratching his face and tearing his clothes on the thorns. But he didn't care, he wanted to be enveloped by the shrubs, totally hidden from view.

Marty unbuckled his pants, slid them down to his ankles, and squatted in the sharp branches, a mere instant before his sphincters blew. Grimacing, he closed his eyes tight and cowered in the bush, tortured by the cramps, the sounds, the smells, and the overpowering humiliation of his nakedness and vulnerability.

Intellectually, Marty knew there was nothing shameful about this. He was a human being. He was ill. He had no choice. But there was nothing he could say to himself to ease his embarrassment, which was even greater than his considerable physical discomfort. Marty pulled the dust mask over his nose, kept his eyes closed, and prayed that no one would walk by as his body convulsed, cramped, and purged.

A wave of heat washed over him, and he was floating, in a fishing boat on Deer Lake, his grandfather holding the rumbling outboard motor with one hand, his eyes on the trolling pole, waiting for a bite.

It was a hot day made even hotter by the reflection of the sun off the aluminum boat. They were a frying pan drifting back-and-forth across the stagnant water. Nobody built homes on Deer Lake. They parked them and put a picnic table in front of the door and called them fishing cabins.

"I have to go to the bathroom," Marty whined for the sixth or seventh time, rocking on his bench, sunburned and uncomfortable, his arms wrapped around his stomach.

His Grandfather, Poppa Earl, held out a rusted MJB coffee can to him. It was full of cigar stubs and ashes, fish guts and peanut shells. "Piss in this. The fish are biting."

"I can't," Marty smelled like a coconut, sweating off the gobs of Coppertone his Mother made him put on every time he went on the lake. "It's number two."

"Then you can hold it a while longer," Poppa Earl decided, absently picking dried fish scales off his pants, while keeping his eyes on the line. "We're on top of a school of silvers. They'll be hopping in the boat soon."

They'd have to. The last fish they caught was three hours ago, and it was a thin, sickly one that probably swallowed the hook on purpose to end his miserable life. They hadn't had a bite since.

"We can go in for a minute and come right back out," Marty argued. "The fish will still be here."

Poppa Earl shot him a furious glance. "You can't catch fish with your line in the boat."

That was Poppa Earl's all-purpose observation on everything in life, from his brother's impotence to the invasion of Grenada, a line of inarguable wisdom that took on even greater, almost religious significance when, in fact, he was actually fishing. When Poppa Earl made that statement, ten-year-old Marty knew no amount of whining, begging, or cajoling would change his mind. So Marty just sat there, staring at the dead fish in the Styrofoam cooler, floating in the bloody ice water.

When Marty couldn't hold it any longer, when he was sobbing with shame as his bowels emptied into his bathing trunks, Poppa Earl was too busy to notice. He'd gotten a bite. Poppa Earl was standing up in the boat, reeling in the leaded line, giving his standard play-by-play the whole time.

"It's bending the pole in half, look at that! It's a monster! It's got to be the killer mack, biggest fish in the lake. They're hungry bastards. I once caught a thirty pound mackinaw on ten-pound test line. Did I ever tell you that? Nearly pulled me out of the boat. But I got him. Oh yes, that fish met his match in me. I'm the nightmare of the dark waters, you know that? For sixty years, I've been coming and killing. They fear me. It's instinct in them now, part of their fish DNA. Whoa, this one is fighting! Don't he know who he's up against?"

And on and on it went, Poppa Earl oblivious to Marty's plight until the six-inch silver, every bit as thin and sickly as the one they caught hours ago, was in the boat and Poppa Earl was back on his bench, yanking the hook out of the fish along with most of his internal organs.

"Lookee there," Poppa Earl held up the fish's stomach between two fingers. "He's been eating somebody's white corn. Who the hell uses white corn for bait?"

Poppa Earl tossed the fish into the cooler and the guts overboard, and was washing his hands in the lake when he sniffed something foul. "What the hell is that smell?"

Marty couldn't look at him. He just hugged himself, trying to become as small as he could, sobbing quietly.

"Did you just shit yourself?" Poppa Earl yelled, rising to his feet. "God-damn it, the fish are biting!"

Poppa Earl picked up Marty under the armpits and threw him into the lake. His grandfather sat back down in front of the outboard, wiped his hands on his pants, and steered the boat back the direction they came.

"You can't catch fish with your line in the boat," his grandfather said, shaking his head disgustedly as the boat chortled off.

T he water was cold and light as mist. It smelled of pine and hospitals and clean counter-tops. He was swimming in a lake of Lysol.

Marty opened his eyes and was blasted in the face again with disinfectant. Someone was holding a can of Lysol out of the window above the hedge, dousing the bush with spray. Before he could say anything—not that he could in his present disoriented, poisoned, and disinfected state—the spraying stopped and an old lady stuck her head out, her smile revealing a row of blazingly white false teeth. Around her withered neck, she wore fake pearls the size of jawbreakers and as white as her teeth. It was all hurting his eyes.

"I hope you're feeling better." Her voice was filtered through a mile of gravel road. "I've got a nice glass of ginger ale and some saltines for you in the courtyard. The gate is open, be sure to close it behind you when you come in."

She dropped a roll of toilet paper into the bush and disappeared. Marty was mortified, but not so much so that he didn't quickly clean himself off, hitch up his pants, and escape from the bush, carrying the rest of the toilet paper roll with him.

He tumbled out of the junipers and tried to regain his balance, feeling as if he just got off a ride on the Tilt-A-Whirl. Everything was spinning, but at least the cramps were gone. He wandered around the corner to the front of the 1940s-era, white-stucco apartment building.

The courtyard was secured behind a wrought iron gate that nearly reached up to the Disney-esque, second-floor turrets on either side of the entrance. Marty went through the gate, closed it behind him, and discovered a lushly landscaped garden, with potted flowers and bird feeders everywhere, the elegant patio furniture arranged around a small pond and a stilled fountain.

"Over here, sweetie." The old lady was waiting for him in a one-piece bathing suit at one of the tables, her bony legs crossed, nervously shaking one foot, the sole of her house slippers slapping against her heel.

Her skin was unnaturally weather-beaten and creased with use; it looked like someone had stretched a loud floral bathing suit over the cracked leather driver's seat of an old car, then strung a necklace of enormous fake pearls around the headrest.

"Come, sit down, before the ginger ale goes flat in this heat," she motioned to the pitcher and two plastic glasses, which were on the table beside some suntan lotion and a beaten-up John Grisham paperback.

Marty took a seat and stared at her as if she was an apparition. The air itself was shimmering like a TV signal that refused to come into focus. All he could do was lamely offer her the roll of toilet paper back.

"You keep it sweetie," she waved her hand at him, each finger ringed with an enormous glass jewel. "In case you have more tummy troubles."

Either he was dying, he thought, or this is just what the body does after riding a fireball, getting shot, and running through a cloud of toxic gas. In which case, shitting his guts out and losing any sense of physical or mental equilibrium would be totally normal and healthy.

Marty set the toilet paper down on the table and reached for the pitcher of ginger ale, but had a hard time capturing it because it wouldn't stay still. Nothing would. He finally managed to grab the pitcher and pour some soda into his glass, but he had real trouble getting any in his mouth, spilling half of it down his shirt before he realized he was still wearing the dust mask. He tore the mask off his face and swallowed the tepid, lukewarm ginger ale in one, long gulp.

It felt good. He immediately filled the glass again, drank it all, then settled back in his seat. The air was rich with the scent of fresh-blooming flowers and a hint of coconuts. For the first time in hours, he felt at peace. Safe. He could stay here forever.

"It's very peaceful here," he said.

"Are you feeling better?"

"Much better, thank you." Enough to feel embarrassed again for what he had done. "I'm sorry about your bush."

"Bushes are ugly things," she said. "I don't care about bushes."

"Why did you help me?"

"We don't get many guests here at the Seville," she took a saltine and swallowed it whole in her huge mouth. "And it's such a nice day."

If this was a nice day, he couldn't imagine what her bad days were like.

"Besides," she smiled, "we entertainment professionals have to stick together."

"How did you know I'm in the TV business?"

"Your bag," she tipped her head towards his gym bag, which had the network logo on the side. "I've done many fine productions for your network."

"What do you do?"

"I'm a featured player," she reached over to the seat beside her and lifted up a huge photo album. "I've been in hundreds of productions and worked with all the major stars."

Marty had absolutely no idea what a featured player was, but at least now he knew why she rescued him from having to wipe his ass with a leaf. Even though her true intentions were revealed, he didn't feel in any hurry to leave. He still felt light-headed and the solitude of her courtyard was soothing.

She opened her album on the table and turned it around to face Marty. "That's me in *Hello Dolly* with Barbara Streisand."

She tapped her gnarled, bejeweled finger on a photo of a crowd outside a train station. "I'm the pretty woman standing behind Walter Matthau."

Before Marty could find her in the picture, she flipped the page to a still from *Planet of the Apes*. "That's me, the monkey woman holding the basket of fruit, two monkeys to the left of the marvelous Edward G. Robinson, though you can't really tell it's him with that make-up on. It was one of my richest roles."

Now Marty understood what the term "featured player" meant. It was either an antiquated description of what she did, or a phrase she made up to make her work seem more like genuine acting. She was an extra, one of the countless, nameless background faces hired at $70 a day plus meals to fill out corridors, streets, and crowd scenes in shows.

She flipped rapidly through the pages. "I left the business after being a nurse for a few seasons on *Diagnosis Murder*. My character just wasn't challenging any more. Most of the time, she walked up and down the same corridor holding the same files. I really felt my character should be answering phones, perhaps even consulting in the background with other physicians. The second assistant director wasn't willing to take the creative risk so I resigned. I've been waiting for the right role for a comeback."

"I see," Marty nodded. "I'm afraid I have nothing to do with the casting of featured players."

"But you'll keep an eye open for any interesting roles?"

"Certainly." Getting her a job as an extra was easy. It was the least he could do for her. He was grateful for her kindness. Then again, he thought about what she might say on the set. Oh, he's a delightful man. I met him when he was shitting in my juniper bushes.

Perhaps he'd just send her a lovely fruit basket instead. Or some flowers for her garden.

"You live here by yourself?" he asked to change the subject.

"Oh no. The Flannerys are upstairs and Mr. Cathburt is relaxing over there," she waved to someone on the other side of the pond.

Marty craned his neck and saw two bare feet and part of a mangled chaise lounge sticking out from under a massive slab of stucco, tile, and glass. The startling sight seemed to sharpen his vision, enough to finally notice that the roof on the second floor had caved in. When he turned back to the old lady, the air wasn't shimmering nearly as much and his pulse was pounding in his head. Death, and the fear of dying, brought things into focus once again.

"Mr. Cathburt likes to take a little nap in the afternoon," she whispered.

"I don't think he's napping."

Marty got up and hurried over to the crushed chaise lounge to see if there was anything he could do for Mr. Cathburt. There wasn't.

Mr. Cathburt was smashed under the remains of a second-floor veranda. On the patio, a few inches away, a glass of iced tea sat undisturbed on the latest issue of The Globe, which was crusted in a dried puddle of blood. The iced tea was cloudy with particles of plaster and stucco, and the headline on The Globe shrieked: Inside Clarissa Blake's Lesbian Love Den! Her Bisexual Galpals Revealed! As curious as Marty was about Clarissa and her galpals, he wasn't about to touch the magazine.

"When he wakes up, Mr. Cathburt and I usually water the garden," the old lady was just chattering away. "Everything would die if it was left up to the Flannerys."

Marty heard another voice, barely audible. At first he thought it might be Mr. Cathburt, squeaking from underneath the veranda, but then he recognized the scratchy broadcast cadence: the voice was coming from a speaker. He looked around and found a tiny head-set dangling from a cord that was pinched between the rubble and the smashed chaise lounge. Somewhere under all that, a Walkman had survived. The cord was sticky with blood, but Marty's desire to hear some news was stronger than his revulsion. He crouched beside the late Mr. Cathburt, picked up the head set, and held it close to his ear.

The newscaster's voice was weak and quivering, as if he was fighting himself to speak at all.

". . . total, catastrophic devastation. The destruction is simply indescribable. The death toll is surely in the thousands. We don't have details because the city has gone dark, there's no electricity, the phone lines are down, all we know is what we're seeing from our traffic chopper and picking up on the police band. We do know the epicenter was somewhere around Chatsworth, and damage extends as far north as Santa Barbara and as far south as San Juan Capistrano. There have been two strong aftershocks and dozens of smaller ones.

The coastal communities of Santa Monica, Marina Del Rey, and Playa Del Rey have been decimated. Wildfires are raging in Baldwin Hills, Malibu, and above Sherman Oaks. City Hall, the Griffith Park Observatory, the UCLA Medical Center, Dodger Stadium, the Santa Monica Pier, and Sleeping Beauty's Castle are a few of the prominent structures that have crumbled. We're hearing widespread reports of chemical spills and explosions, landslides, and bridge collapses. Underground gas lines have broken, fueling intense firestorms that have razed neighborhoods in Chatsworth, the Fairfax district, and Culver City.

Every freeway has sustained massive damage and most major streets are impassable, drastically impeding official rescue efforts, which are sporadic at best right now.

Los Angeles International Airport is on fire, its runways destroyed. Van Nuys Airport and Santa Monica Airport have also suffered severe damage.

The National Guard has been called in, but with virtually no way into the city, it could be days before they arrive in significant numbers.

We are on our own . . ."

Marty dropped the headset, his hand shaking. He was scared. There was no news about Calabasas, his home, but he didn't take any relief in that. Calabasas wasn't far from the epicenter of the quake and more than once had been threatened by fires that spread from Malibu canyon. Was their house destroyed? Was his wife about to be consumed by a raging wildfire?

"We spend the whole day out here, Mr. Cathburt and I, reading mostly," the old lady was still talking. "It took Mr. Cathburt three weeks to read *The Pelican Brief*. I finished it in a weekend, but I'm not like most people. I like literary fiction."

"You should go," Marty got up quickly and went to her. "It isn't safe here. The rest of this building could come down."

"I have all the John Grisham books, if you'd like to borrow one. We could read here together, by the pond."

The garden didn't seem nearly so peaceful anymore. Now he could hear the flies buzzing over Mr. Cathburt, the wailing car alarms on the street, the thup-thup-thup of a helicopter in the distance, the tingle of bits of glass still falling to the ground.

"I have to go," Marty told the old woman. "You should, too."

"Where would I go?" she looked him in the eye. "I've lived here for forty-seven years. There is no where else. This is my garden."

Marty nodded. "Is there anything I can do for you before I go?"

"Yes, please." She slid the straps of her bathing suit off her shoulders and smiled coyly.

Oh God, no, Marty thought.

She handed him the bottle of Hawaiian Tropic. "I could use some suntan lotion on my back."

Marty didn't want to do it, but he was so relieved that was all she was asking, he quickly squirted some lotion on his hands, rubbed them together, and smoothed the cream on her shoulders. It felt like he was polishing a dashboard with Armor All.

"That feels so good," she purred. "Your hands are very soft."

"You shit in her bushes," said a familiar voice, "that doesn't mean you've got to fuck her."

Marty turned and was stunned to see Buck leaning against the courtyard gate, shaking his head in disgust. Wasn't there any way to escape this guy?

"To each his own, I suppose," Buck shrugged and left.

"Thank you again for your help," Marty hurriedly wiped his hands on his jacket, realizing too late that now he'd be carrying that coconut scent with him the rest of his journey. Then again, it beat the scent he'd been carrying so far.

"Come back and visit any time," she smiled. "And keep your eyes open for the right script for me."

He forced a smile in return, took the toilet paper, and left, closing the gate behind him.

CHAPTER SEVEN
The Mythic Hero Paradigm

Buck was waiting for him on the curb.

"Your running is improving," Buck said. "It would be more impressive, however, if you didn't shit yourself the minute you stopped."

"Can we change the subject?" Marty started walking, stuffing the toilet paper into his pack as he went.

"Okay," Buck fell into step beside him. "Let's talk about breasts."

"Let's talk about why you're following me."

"If you weren't so fucking full of yourself, asshole, you'd remember that I live in Hollywood. We happen to be going in the same direction."

"There are at least a dozen different ways of getting to Hollywood."

"Not if you want to avoid the giant fucking cloud of poison fucking gas. Besides, I'm getting to like you, Mark."

"Martin. You won't like me so much after I tell the police what you did."

"I'm sure it will be a top priority for them." Buck snorted.

"You were supposed to stay with the guy you shot."

Buck grinned. "I'm with you now, aren't I?"

"The other guy you shot."

"Enrique and the black kid are with him. Turns out Enrique is one of those male nurses which, as we all know, means he's an amateur proctologist in his spare time."

Marty gave him a look, took the map out of his pack, and spread it on the hood of a car.

"What are you doing?" Buck asked.

"Trying to figure out where I am."

"You're a couple blocks away from Koreatown," Buck said. "Keep heading west, and we'll hit Western Boulevard."

"How can you tell?" Marty glanced around for a street sign, finally spotting one lying on the ground.

"Because I live here, asshole. Don't you ever look out the window when you drive?"

"I don't drive here." Marty studied the map for the street and discovered Buck was right. They were on the northern edge of Koreatown. It could be the safest stretch of his journey or the most dangerous, all because of another violent upheaval not so long ago.

In the early hours of the Rodney King riots, while news choppers hovered over the streets, scores of enraged blacks surged through Koreatown, looting, torching, and demolishing storefronts and mini-malls. It was an unstoppable tide of furious humanity and terrific TV.

Although the Koreans had nothing to do with the beating of Rodney or the acquittal of the officers involved, they were resented for opening their liquor stores, markets, and gas stations in black communities and not hiring blacks.

The besieged Koreans quickly armed themselves, gun-toting brigades patrolling the streets while others stood guard on the rooftops, cradling their carbines, watching and waiting for the invaders to return. But it was too late; the Koreans had already suffered nearly half the damage inflicted on the city during the riots.

Still, Marty was quick to see the series potential. Immediately after the riots, he developed a pilot entitled *LA Seoul*, about vigilante Koreans cleaning up the mean streets. It didn't make the schedule, despite a last minute attempt to rework it for the Olsen twins. Instead, the network bought *Cross-Eyed*, a show about a born-again private eye taking cases from God.

The Koreans certainly hadn't forgotten the riots and were probably back on the streets, armed against another incursion. Which meant the neighborhood might be safe from looters but teeming with trigger-happy vigilantes hostile to any strangers, even one who championed what could have been the first Korean cop show on primetime television.

Marty decided having Buck around might not be so bad after all, at least until he got to the Cahuenga Pass and was on his way into the valley. He folded up his map and stuck it in his inside jacket pocket.

"So, once we get to Hollywood, you'll be home," Marty said. "Right?"

"Yeah."

"And we go our separate ways."

"That's a cliché," Buck said. "Something that's been said so many fucking times it means shit."

"Yes, I know what a cliché is, thank you." It was going to be a long walk to Hollywood.

5 :35 p.m. Tuesday

Marty and Buck were in a place where people worshipped wrought iron. It surrounded their properties, covered their windows, and barred their doors. It made them feel safe. Now, the wrought iron fences were all that was standing around their homes, which had crumbled like stale cake.

If only their homes had been made of wrought iron, Marty thought.

"The ones I hate are the pointy kind, the ones that seem to be going two different directions," Buck said. "Like they're trying to get the hell off her body or something."

"What are you talking about?"

"Breasts," Buck replied. "As in tits, jugs, and honkers."

"Thanks for the clarification."

"I changed the subject, like you asked. Try to keep up."

And as Buck prattled on, Marty shifted his attention to the ruins around them.

They passed a large apartment building, its outer walls stripped away so it looked like the set of *The Hollywood Squares*. Except instead of seeing celebrities sitting behind desks, answering stupid questions, Marty saw unmade beds and overturned chairs, fallen pictures in shattered frames, kitchens splattered with broken dishware and spilled food.

The Korean tenants were scavenging what they could, despite the strong possibility the building could collapse right on top of them. Four bloodied tenants struggled to heft a dented Kenmore dishwasher out of a ground floor apartment. Other tenants carefully carted out computers, stereo systems, and TVs, gathering it all on the sidewalk under the guard of family members.

It didn't matter that these goodies were useless to them now, that they wouldn't keep them alive, warm, and healthy for another day. What was important is what they'd once cost. A can of corn and the water it was packed with was only worth sixty-five cents, a dishwasher was worth three hundred dollars. At that price, who cared if the machine worked or if you'd live to use it again?

Yet even as Marty watched them, shaking his head with disdain, he found himself wondering if Beth managed to retrieve his laptop and their new TiVo. Before he could berate himself, they reached Western Avenue, which looked like it had been plowed up the center by an enormous hoe. Cars, buses and telephone poles were scattered everywhere, overturned by the uplifted roadway.

The street was filled with people, mostly Koreans, treating their wounds, embracing each other, or staring in dazed disbelief at the destruction. Marty hardly noticed; the scene had become the only familiar site in this transformed city, the new standard of normalcy. The only people who caught Marty's attention were the ones holding AK-47s, standing in front of their slumped storefronts and flattened mini-malls, just waiting for the looting hordes to arrive.

Marty looked over at Buck, worried that the Neanderthal psycho might do something. "Don't do anything stupid, Buck. Let's just walk through here as quietly and as inconspicuously as we can. We don't want trouble."

"What the fuck are you afraid I'm going to do?"

"I don't know, but these people are very nervous and the slightest thing might set them off."

"They don't look nervous to me."

"Then why are they holding automatic weapons?"

"So you'll be nervous," Buck waved to the nearest armed Korean. "Yang chow, amigo-san."

Marty averted his gaze and hurried along as fast as he could. He didn't want to be too close when the Korean gunned down Buck.

Koreatown was nothing like the one Marty remembered from LA Seoul, which was claustrophobic, humid, and dark, the air thick with incense and opium and dangerous men in Manchu jackets. Nor, much to Marty's surprise, was this Koreatown packaged for tourists yet, the entire country and culture synthesized into Disneyfied pagodas and imitation silk robes with catchy slogans.

The only thing Marty could see that set this bland retail strip apart from any other were the services offered—acupuncture, aromatherapy, Shiatsu massage?and the plethora of signs, all written in bright, red Korean calligraphy with English translations in tiny print underneath.

Shong Hack Dong's Permanent Make-up. Jang Soo Bakery. Myung Ga Massage. Yum Park Sa Ne Restaurant. Yeh's Tailor. Myong Dong Natural Herbs. Kentucky Fried Chicken.

That stopped Marty.

There, unscathed and resplendent amidst the destruction, the smiling caricature of Colonel Sanders smiled down at Marty from atop a sleek building comprised of metal cubes, aerodynamic fins, and steel vents. It looked like the Colonel just returned from outer space with an emergency bucket of extra crispy chicken.

"Good idea, Marty," Buck said. "I was feeling a little hungry myself."

"I don't think it's open."

"Don't worry, the maitre'd knows me." Buck headed for the restaurant.

That's when they heard the shriek of rubber against asphalt. Marty and Buck turned to see a truck, its tires spinning and smoking, pulling a set of chains attached to an ATM machine in the wall of a bank. The front of the truck bucked like a horse, its front tires lifting off the ground; then it landed hard and jumped forward, tearing the ATM out and dragging it a few feet before stopping in a cloud of stucco and loose cash.

Two Mexicans piled out of the truck, grabbed bags from the back of the bed, and started scooping up the cash while a third man watched, a shotgun in his arms.

Marty glanced at the Koreans. They weren't doing anything, even though they had the Mexican out-gunned a hundred to one. They were just standing there, watching. They didn't seem to care at all, which was a great relief to Marty, who didn't want to die in a shootout, but he was curious why they weren't interested.

Then he saw the Wells Fargo sign and understood. It wasn't their bank. Even so, Marty wanted to get going in case they changed their minds. He was about to tell Buck just that when the bounty hunter drew his gun and smiled.

"This will only take a minute," Buck started towards the men.

Marty grabbed him. "What the hell are you doing?"

But Marty already knew, because it was what the moment demanded, playing out just like those $800-a-weekend screenwriting courses and countless action movies said it should. It was the inevitable scene when the hero proves what a wild, dangerous man he is by stumbling into a hold-up, a hostage situation, a guy attempting suicide, or a creative combination of all three.

But this wasn't a movie.

"They're robbing a bank." Buck let his arm hang straight, hiding the weapon behind his leg. "That's a no-no."

"Who gives a shit?" Marty said. "We just had an earthquake. The city has been leveled. The money doesn't matter."

"It will."

Buck shook free of Marty and marched across the street towards the Mexican with the shotgun, who didn't seem to notice him.

Buck yelled: "Hey, Taco Bell!"

Now the Mexican did. He pointed the shotgun at Buck.

"Yeah, you," Buck kept coming. "You think you're slick?"

The self-anointed screenwriting gurus called this the defining moment, or more pompously, "the essential re-stating of the mythic-hero paradigm," and Marty hated it every time he saw it. The moment was false, formulaic, and creatively bankrupt. Yet, Marty demanded that writers give it to him in the first five minutes of the first episode of every cop show on his network. And if they argued with him about doing it, he fired them and brought in a writer who would. Now Marty was being forced by fate, or some cosmic guardian of the Writers Guild of America, to live the scene. Or die from it.

The two unarmed Mexicans stopping shoving cash into their bags and rose to their feet, shared a worried look, and faced Buck. They didn't know what to make of this guy. One of them said something threatening to him in Spanish.

"No habla bullshit, Dorrito," Buck continued to advance on the shooter, who shifted his weight nervously, looking to his friends for guidance and not getting any.

"Fuck off," the shooter told Buck. "Or I shoot."

Buck shook his head and turned to the two unarmed men. "Where'd you guys find this moron?" He motioned to the shooter, and they looked, which distracted them from seeing his gun as he passed by. "Taco Bell doesn't know shit and I can prove it."

The shooter raised his shotgun level with Buck's chest. "I blow your balls off you don't stop."

"Not with the safety on, dipshit."

The shooter glanced down at shotgun. In that instant of inattention, Buck jammed his gun into the man's groin with one hand and swatted the shotgun aside with the other.

Buck leaned into his face so their noses were almost touching. "If your friends don't sit the fuck down and do exactly what they're told, you'll be a Ken doll."

The shooter was either stupidly defiant or simply unfamiliar with what Barbie wanted from a man, because he didn't say a word. So Buck cocked the trigger and pushed the gun into him. "How about this? They sit or Taco Bell is gonna be Tinker Bell."

The point, if not the allusion, got through to the Shooter, who immediately told his friends to sit. They did.

Marty looked at the Koreans. They were smiling. The scene worked every time. It didn't make it any less stupid. Now that the situation seemed to be under control, Marty marched over to Buck and said: "Are you out of your fucking mind?"

"Stop whining and take away Taco Bell's shotgun."

Marty took it from the shooter's hand, examined it, then tossed it into the truck bed. "The safety wasn't on."

Buck grinned at the glowering Mexican. "Oops."

B uck was still grinning after he and Marty finished tying the three Mexicans to a telephone pole. It only made Marty angrier.

"You think it's funny, Buck? You could have gotten killed. And for what?"

"A big, fat paycheck." Buck stuck one of his business cards into in the shirt pocket of each of his prisoners. "When the cops show up, they'll know who caught these dipshits. And so will the bank. I should get a couple grand out of this. You know, this earthquake could be real good for my business."

"Do me a favor, Buck. Take the rest of the day off."

Marty walked away, weaving through the small crowd of Koreans who gathered to watch Buck at work. Buck tipped an imaginary hat at the smiling Koreans and joined Marty.

"What the fuck are you so angry about?"

"Because you could have started a shoot-out back there," Marty replied. "And if one of the Koreans got hit, they'd have started shooting too, and it would have been a bloodbath."

"Bullshit," Buck smiled and pointed an accusatory finger at Marty. "You were worried about me."

"I was afraid I'd get killed and wouldn't make it home to my wife."

"See? It's happening already. You're rooting for me. I told you I was a great fucking character," Buck clapped Marty on the back. "I'm even willing to consider a black sidekick, as long as it's not Arsenio Hall."

Years from now, this was the anecdote Marty would tell at parties or network events. How in the middle of the Big One, climbing through the ruins of LA to get back home, he was pursued by a crazy bounty hunter trying to pitch him a series.

Was that what the big stunt at the bank was all about? Part of the pitch? Whether it was or not, it would be when Marty told the story.

But the story would soon be coming to an end. It was a little after six. Another mile or two, they'd be in Hollywood. Buck would go home, disappearing from his life forever, and Marty would continue over the Cahuenga Pass, arriving in the San Fernando Valley just as night fell. The rest of the trip would be a straight shot down Ventura Boulevard to Calabasas.

Nice and easy. Maybe there would even be a Starbucks open for business. With so many of them in the valley, statistically it just wasn't possible that the Big One had leveled them all.

That pleasant thought occupied Marty for the next half hour as they climbed over rubble and moved through the injured, the lost, and the hopeless.

Marty tried to imagine how Beth would look, how happy she

would be to see him. In his mind, there wasn't a scratch on her, she was as he left her that morning in the kitchen. Only the coldness would be gone, because he knew if he could walk across this decimated city to her, then traveling the distance in their marriage wouldn't seem so hard anymore.

To make that journey, he'd have to start almost two years ago. They weren't living in the Calabasas house then; they were still in the ranch-style place in Reseda. They were "north of the boulevard," the demarcation line across the valley separating those who'd "made it" and were living in the foothills above Ventura Boulevard from those still trying to and living in the flatlands below.

Marty was in his home office, stuck on page 138 of his second, unfinished novel. Shortly after he got his network job, he set aside his unfinished scripts, rationalizing his failure to complete a screenplay was the price he paid for being too damn good at his job. He spent his days developing other people's scripts, criticizing draft after draft until the writers got the story and the characters as good as their limited skills would allow. The problem was when Marty sat down to write himself at night, he couldn't stop being a network executive. He couldn't write a line without giving himself notes before he was even done typing it.

So Marty switched to novels, knowing that would free him up creatively to be the inventive, insightful, prolific writer he knew he was.

Or would be . . . if he could just get past page 138.

It wasn't so much that the stories petered out, which they did, but that none of the characters ever seemed to come to life. They were just game pieces, moving around the plot, performing their story function without ever breathing. He was always dragging them across the page, pushing them into situations, forcing them to speak, and then agonizing over each word they said.

Just once, Marty wanted a character to take over, to say things that surprised him, to take the story in new directions he hadn't thought of until he was actually writing them.

He was in one of those frustrating moments, staring hatefully at his laptop, at that 26,962nd word on the 138th page, when Beth came up behind him and put her hand on his shoulder. She meant to be affectionate and considerate, to disturb him as gently as possible, but the truth was he loathed the interruption no matter how nicely it was done, even when it wasn't interrupting anything.

In fact, especially when it wasn't.

"In two months, we'll have been married three years," Beth said softly.

"I haven't forgotten our anniversary yet, but I appreciate the reminder."

Marty regretted the tone of his voice right away and knew he'd hurt her by the way she let her hand drop off his shoulder. But Beth didn't leave, she just dropped onto his ratty couch, the $200 Levitz special he'd been dragging from one house to another since college, and waited for him to turn around.

He did, and saw her snuggled into one corner, her knees drawn up to her chest, which he knew meant that a serious conversation was coming, and whatever it was, he'd just made it worse. Damage control time.

"I'm sorry," he said. "You caught me at a really bad moment. I'm in a difficult place in my book. The truth is, I'm stuck."

"So am I," she said. "I spend my days either going to auditions or playing bit parts, and my nights studying for them."

"You're an actress, that's what you've got to do. The performance is what it's all about." He wondered what this was leading to, what this had to do with being married for three years, and why she had to bring it up now, on page 138.

"Tomorrow I'm playing a reporter who can't get laid because she's got bad breath but finds the man of her dreams once she starts using an amazing new mouthwash with an incredible, minty taste."

Marty smiled. "It's a beginning. You're working towards something."

"But I'm not getting there," Beth glanced at his laptop. "Neither of us is."

That was the most devastating, hurtful thing she'd ever said to him, even more so because she threw it off so casually, like it was an obvious truth. Which Marty supposed it was, he just had no idea she knew. And now it was out there, the unsaid said. He wasn't a writer.

"You never wanted me to," Marty said. "You were the one who pushed me to take a development job."

"I didn't have to push very hard."

"Is that why you came in here, to tell me I can't write or that you can't act?"

It was what Marty always did when she attacked, strike back even harder. He knew this about himself, and yet he couldn't stop doing it.

She studied her knees, which was a much safer place to be looking right now than at her husband. "No," she replied softly.

That was Beth, winning by not upping the ante. She could get away with being cruel because he always fired back even harder, and then she'd acquiesce. And then he'd feel guilty, and he'd be the one to apologize. Even if he didn't, she still occupied the higher ground. It was a constant, repeated pattern in their conflicts; they both knew it, and neither one seemed able to break it.

The dog came bounding in ready to play, drool-soaked ball in his mouth, but even his dog brain was sophisticated enough to read the vibes in the room. He dropped his ball and slinked right out again.

"Why are we trying so hard?" she asked. "You working all day at the network and then trying to write all night. Me, going after as many parts as I can, taking anything that I'm offered?"

"Because that's what you have to do to make it, to achieve your goals."

"So that's what we are, two people trying to achieve their goals."

"What's wrong with that?"

"It's not enough."

He knew what was missing. What he didn't say. But it wasn't too late to correct the mistake.

"We're also two people who love each other very much." Sometimes the right line came to him in life but rarely in fiction. For most writers, it was the other way around, but he didn't consider himself fortunate.

She smiled, acknowledging his effort. "Two people who love each other but spend every moment in their separate worlds, obsessed with achieving their dreams. And for what?"

"To be who we want to be."

"If that's all it is, then it's selfish and it's empty and it's lonely. We should be working for something, something shared."

"Your success will make me as happy as it makes you," he said. "Maybe more so, because I want it so badly for you. That makes it shared."

"That's sweet, and probably the perfect thing to say, but it doesn't change anything. The fact is we're doing it for ourselves. Not for us, not for our marriage, not for our family. If it was, then it would be worth it."

Our family? What family?

And then he knew what this was all about, a long-winded, philosophical way of saying what could be expressed directly in four words. So he said them.

"You want a baby."

She shook her head. "I want a family."

Marty turned back to his laptop, giving himself some space to think. If he couldn't write now, how much easier would it be with a wailing baby in the house? Forget the sleep deprivation, the noise, the demands on his time. What about the responsibility of having a child? The terror alone was enough to smother what little creative impulses he had left.

There he was being selfish again, Marty scolded himself. He wasn't thinking of her or of their marriage, only his personal goals. Isn't that exactly what Beth was talking about? Marty knew it was, but he also knew he didn't feel the least bit guilty about it, or any less in love with her. He didn't want to lose her, but he wasn't ready to give up on himself just yet.

"Do we have to decide right now?" he asked.

"Soon." She got up, kissed him on the top of his head, and walked out.

And a few months later, 138 pages into another novel, in the middle of a screening of his wife's bit part in a movie, a bit of Christopher Walkan in a part of his wife, Marty decided he was ready for kids.

And a few months after that, Marty discovered he was no better at creating a character in the womb than he was on the page.

Buck elbowed him in the ribs, intruding on his thoughts. "You think that's an after-quake special or their regular price?"

Marty followed his gaze and saw a sign dangling from a half-crumbled, stone wall. It read: Complete Funeral Service with steel or wood casket only $988 at Hollywood Park Cemetery . . . Hollywood Forever."

"What do they give you for a headstone at that price? An index card?" Buck snorted and shook his head.

Marty was stunned, not by the sign, but by the fact he was

standing at the gates of the Hollywood Park Cemetery. He figured he must have walked the last couple miles in some kind of trance, letting himself be led by Buck, because he had no memory of leaving Western Avenue and trudging down Santa Monica Boulevard. But here they were, outside the eternal backlot, where Jayne Mansfield, Tyrone Power, Harry Cohn, Rudolph Valentino, and Cecil B. DeMille were buried under the shadow of the Paramount Studios soundstages, which abutted the southern edge of the cemetery.

The cemetery had become a tent city, hundreds of people seeking refuge among the toppled tombstones and crumbled crypts, finding some measure of safety in the open space of the dead.

But Marty wasn't looking at them. His gaze was fixed on the Paramount water tower, looming over the studio soundstages and the cemetery. To him, the water tower was like a palm tree in a desert oasis. Seeing it gave Marty a real sense of relief and security, as if he'd already arrived home.

Marty was one of the industry elite with a permanent Paramount gate pass. He could go on the lot whenever he pleased, dine in the private commissary, stroll down the fake city streets, and make unannounced visits to the offices of the most powerful writers, producers, and executives in the business.

He wanted to run through the studio gates right now, take a shower in a mobile dressing room, get a fresh suit of clothes from the wardrobe department, and then sit the disaster out in safety, sipping a mineral water and snacking on fresh fruit. He wouldn't have to walk any more, to turn his face away from the injured and the dead. They would be on the other side of the walls.

With Beth.

Maybe injured. Maybe dead.

He turned away from the water tower and faced north, where the Hollywood sign, or more accurately, the three crooked letters that remained of it, was visible through the smoke and dust that hung above the canted palm trees and listing office towers.

That was where he had to go.

Marty pushed on, heading up the gradual slope of Gower Street towards Sunset Boulevard, the Hollywood Hills, and the valley beyond. A few blocks ahead of him, he could see smoke rising from vehicles piled up on the Hollywood Freeway over-crossing.

He wouldn't risk going under the concrete span, he'd cross west on Franklin instead, then follow Highland north alongside the freeway through the Cahuenga Pass until the avenue dropped into the valley and transformed into Ventura Boulevard.

"When we get to my place, if it's still standing, I got to show you my bathroom," Buck came up beside Marty. "I wallpapered it with cocktail napkins I collected from bars all over the country. Babes love it."

Marty looked at him incredulously. "Really?"

"All it takes is a stapler and some varnish and you're in fuck city."

"When this is all over, instead of rebuilding the Hollywood sign, maybe that's what they should write on those hills," Marty swept his hand in front of him, laying the words out boldly across the sky. "Fuck City."

"I got a note on that," Buck said. "It's gotta say Fucked City."

That was a note Marty couldn't argue with.

CHAPTER EIGHT
The Poseidon Adventure

6:47 p.m. Tuesday
In the movie *Earthquake*, the Capitol Records building was one of the first to collapse, toppling like the stack of LPs it was designed to represent. But there it was, still standing, two blocks up from where Marty and Buck were, in the intersection of Sunset and Vine. One more thing the movies got wrong.

Uprooted palm trees were tipped at crazy angles or lay broken across the Sunset Boulevard, cars piled up against them or crushed underneath. The Cinerama Dome theatre, to Marty's left, was riddled with cracks and resembled half of a discarded eggshell. To his right, the Quantum Insurance office tower rose from a courtyard of broken glass, which the setting sun transformed into a field of glittering diamonds. It was almost beautiful. But Marty kept a wary eye on the tower, afraid it might topple at any moment.

Buck tipped his head towards the Cinerama Dome. "I live over there, on Yucca. Just a few blocks over."

"It's out of my way," Marty motioned towards the Capitol Records building. "I'm heading north."

"What about my bathroom?"

"I really want to get home. My wife is waiting for me."

Buck nodded. "Yeah, well, Thor is probably anxious to see me, too."

"Thor?"

"Yeah, Thor. My fucking dog," Buck looked genuinely hurt. "Haven't you listened to anything I've told you?"

Was this guy for real? Marty thought. Did Buck really think he was hanging on his every word?

"Forgive me, I've been a bit distracted. You know, with the earthquake, hanging from overpasses, that kind of thing."

"Right, whatever." Buck pulled out his gun and, for an instant, Marty was afraid he was going to get shot again.

"You want it?" Buck offered him the gun. "Strictly as a loaner."

"What would I do with a gun?"

"Shoot people, dipshit. It's only gonna get worse out here."

"No thanks," Marty replied. "I wouldn't want to deprive you of the opportunity to pick off a few more looters."

"I got plenty of guns at home."

"I'm sure you do. But really, I don't need it."

"You're making a fatal mistake," Buck shoved the gun back into his holster and held out his hand to Marty. "If you survive, we'll do lunch."

Marty shook it, not out of any sort of friendship, but in an effort to speed Buck on his way. He never wanted to see this man again. "Sure, that would be great."

Buck nodded and strode off down the street. Marty watched him go until he lost him in the crowd. He wanted to make sure Buck wasn't going to follow him any more.

Satisfied that he was truly on his own, Marty continued on up the street, a new determination in his stride. This was a turning point in his journey, and a positive one at that.

When Marty set out on his trek that morning, he didn't anticipate Molly, Buck, Franklin, the bum, or the old lady with vinyl skin. There were no explosions or rescues, toxic clouds, or uncontrollable bowels in his scenario. But despite all that, Marty was where he wanted to be, roughly on schedule. The worst of his ordeal was behind him.

Martin Slack was finally on top of the situation, a man in charge of his destiny. And he enjoyed that terrific feeling, in all of its richness, for a full fifteen seconds.

And then came the aftershock.

His first thought, in the instant he both heard and felt the massive subterranean thunderclap, was that he'd become a joke in a cruel, celestial sitcom. He would never dare think he was in control of his life again.

Marty stood in place, trying to maintain his balance as the ground undulated beneath his feet, the terrified screams of the people scrambling around him muffled by the heavy, sonorous rumble of destruction. Buildings seemed to melt into the ground. Huge fissures moved up the street, ripping the asphalt open like zippers. Glass splashed like raindrops onto the rippling sidewalks.

But just as the shaking began to ebb, he heard a tremendous roar, something so deep and so sustained it overwhelmed the earth's rumble in sound and in motion, growing in intensity and resonance as it came closer.

Yes, closer.

That was Marty's first, intuitive warning that this was something different. It wasn't like the quake, which he felt all over, all at once. This was coming, strong and ferocious, from the hills.

And then he saw it, and for the longest second of his life, was so awe-struck by its horrific magnitude that he couldn't move.

A gigantic wave of water, roiling with mud, trees, cars, power lines, and entire houses, surged over the Hollywood Freeway and smashed into the Columbia Records building, absorbing the rubble in its ferocious maelstrom.

Marty ran screaming in terror, knowing there was no escape, no higher ground, that in seconds he would be buried under a liquid avalanche of rubble, muck, and corpses.

The Quantum Insurance building loomed in front of him, and he rushed into it because it was there, because he could hear the roar of the water and feel its muddy spray as it gained on him. Only then, as he ran across the lobby, and saw the open door to the stairwell, did he have an idea of how he might save himself.

He dashed into the stairwell and scaled the metal steps as fast as he could. The wave pounded into the building, rocking it like a boat, jolting Marty off his feet. He grabbed hold of the rail and kept climbing as water burst into the stairwell from the lobby, a swirling, dark mass rising up for him.

Marty scurried frantically up the stairs, barely ahead of the surging waters. The building continued to shudder as the water, and the enormous chunks of debris, continued to slam against it.

Suddenly, the doors above him exploded open, thick water pouring down the stairs, swamping him in a muck of debris that felt like a stream of razor blades, slicing his clothes, his skin.

Marty screamed in frustration and terror, slipping and sliding on the slick metal steps, desperately afraid of falling and being sucked into the whirlpool chasing him up the stairwell.

A desk chair shot through an open doorway above him, propelled by the water, and tumbled towards his head. He flattened himself against the rail and it banged off the walls past him, splashing into the churning muck and disappearing below. He kept climbing, as fast as he could, his screams like a cheering squad, driving him on, driving up and up and up.

File cabinets and desks piled up against the doorways as he passed, clogging them, slowing the streams of water coursing into the stairwell. He just kept screaming and climbing until finally, he passed doorways where no water at all was coming out.

Marty stopped and risked a look back. Several flights below, the churning monster had given up its pursuit and even seemed to be slowly retreating. Panting, soaked, and bleeding, he slumped down onto a step to catch his breath and stare down at the water.

A woman's face bubbled up out of the morass, eyes wide, skin bulging. He yelped and staggered back.

Beth.

It couldn't be. He blinked hard and looked again, just as the severed torso bobbed up onto the surface. She wasn't his wife, she was another young woman, perhaps the meaning of some other man's journey. She was a woman once loved by someone, now just a piece of floating debris, already starting to rot away. No one would ever find her, no one would ever know what happened. No one except him, and he didn't even know her name.

Marty continued up the stairs, unable to take his eyes off the mutilated corpse, until it finally lolled over, face down in the water. He backed out through the first doorway he came to, and found himself in the seventh floor lobby of Quantum Insurance.

Standing there, amidst the wood paneling and leather furniture, staring at the open, stairwell door, Marty could almost believe that what just happened was merely a waking nightmare, a delusion.

It wasn't possible to drown in an office building stairwell. How could it have nearly happened to him?

But his soaked clothes, the sting of his cuts, the smell of rot already coming from the stairwell, reinforced what he knew was true.

It did happen. A mountain of water roared down Vine Street and chased him up the stairs of a building.

And he'd survived.

He'd beaten it.

He was Charlton Fucking Heston.

Air whistled through the lobby, kicking up papers, magazines, and plaster dust, catching his attention. He turned from the stairwell and stumbled into the offices. Fluorescent light fixtures, tangled in fallen ceiling panels, dangled over the rows of toppled cubicles. Forgotten briefcases, purses, and jackets were scattered everywhere, evidence of a quick evacuation.

Maybe if he searched the purses, Marty thought, he'd find the woman in the stairwell. Or maybe she wasn't from this building or even this block, maybe she was swept off her front lawn miles away and carried down from the hills, her body tossed and dismembered in the swirling waters.

Marty told himself to stop thinking about her, put her in that place in his mind where Molly already was. Close the door and try to barricade it behind the useless mental clutter of restaurant phone numbers, advertising jingles, and the names of cartoon characters.

As Marty moved down the wide corridor, he peeked into the abandoned offices, which looked as if they'd been ransacked, the windows gone, wind whipping in and tossing up the mess.

Windows.

It suddenly occurred to Marty that he was high above the destruction, that if he wanted to, he could see what awaited him on the ground. He carefully made his way into one of the corner offices, afraid he might trip on something and fall out the big opening.

What he saw made him dizzy, made him reach out to the wall for support. The enormity of the devastation was almost too much for his brain to absorb.

The Hollywood Dam had collapsed, spilling the Lake Hollywood Reservoir out into the city, washing away the hillside and all the homes on it. The avalanche of water wiped away the Hollywood Freeway and buried the mouth of the Cahuenga Pass before spreading out into city below, scraping off entire blocks in its wave of debris.

The force of the water, thick with the rubble it had sucked up, dissipated the wider it spread and the more obstacles it hit, thinning out over an ever-widening plain of ruin. Piles of assorted wreckage (mangled swingsets, twisted lightpoles, chunks of freeway lanes, entire buses—were washed up against the tallest buildings, caught against them like seaweed and driftwood as the water streamed past).

Marty quickly moved from one office to another, checking the views out the windows, racing to see as much as he could before the details were swallowed up in the smoke, dust, and near-darkness that was rapidly enveloping the city.

The water was still moving, thinning out to a trickle in a wide "V" that stretched to Western on the East and La Brea to the West, and as far south as Melrose. Helicopters swarmed over Hollywood now, search-lights raking the flood plain, searching for survivors or taking measure of the futility of the effort.

And then Marty realized that somewhere under all the mud and debris clogging the streets was Buck Weaver, his guns, his dog, and his collection of cocktail napkins. Marty couldn't help but imagine Buck, facing off defiantly against the wave, daring it to come for him, firing his gun pointlessly into the wall of water and screaming obscenities at it. He felt a strong, almost physical sadness, and it surprised him.

Marty had only known the guy a few hours, and what he knew about Buck he didn't like. So why were there tears in his eyes?

Their relationship, if it could even be called that, wasn't *The Odd Couple*. There was no hidden affection at the center of their conflict. Buck was a danger to them both and Marty was glad when he finally got rid of him. But Marty never wanted him to die.

Two people he'd met today, actually talked to and got to know in some small way, were dead. Perhaps that was what the tears were all about, he thought. The shock of immediate death and the realization that it could just as easily happen to him.

Maybe it wasn't sadness he felt. It was fear.

Whatever it was, it was overpowering, crippling, and he had to get past it, or he would never be able to leave the building.

He thought again about Beth, about how important it was to get back to her. She was his center. He told himself that as long as he concentrated on her, he could get past any emotion, any obstacle.

Obstacles.

Marty looked out the window again. There was no way he was going to get through the Cahuenga Pass now. He would have to find another way to get over the hills into the valley.

The reason he'd chosen the Cahuenga Pass, besides the fact it was his nearest escape route, was that it was a wide expanse of generally flat land through the hills, there were no dangerous cliffs to worry about, and he could stay clear of unstable slopes that might collapse on him in an aftershock. He also had three routes to choose from through the Pass: Highland Avenue, Cahuenga Boulevard, or the Hollywood Freeway.

There were several canyons that snaked through the hills into the valley, but they didn't offer the same advantages as the Cahuenga Pass. They were all narrow, winding, and crammed with homes clinging precariously to the sides of the canyon. Long stretches of roadway were cut into slopes, leaving a steep drop on the other side. One landslide, one sheared-off chunk of road, and he'd have to turn back.

To the northwest, immense clouds of dust hung over Laurel Canyon, a sign that landslides had probably already closed off that route for him or, at the very least, made it too risky to attempt. And Marty could see the glow from the fires raging in the hills above Sherman Oaks, raising the ominous possibility that even if the other canyons were clear, they soon might be choked off by flames.

There were two other ways into the valley. He could follow the San Diego Freeway and Sepulveda Boulevard through the Sepulveda Pass or, as a last resort, follow the Pacific Coast Highway north, then cut across either Topanga Canyon or Malibu Canyon.

But one, frustrating fact was certain: whichever route Marty eventually chose, he wouldn't be making it back to Calabasas tonight.

It would be a few hours at least before the water receded and he could even attempt leaving the building, much less slogging through the mud, the rubble, and the bodies on the streets. And even if he could, did he really want to do that in the pitch darkness of a blacked-out, demolished metropolis?

A horrible thought came to him. Come daylight, there would be hundreds of corpses. Mutilated. Bloated. Strewn everywhere, washed up by the flood. Marty didn't think he had enough corners in his mind to hide all the death he was going to see. He doubted anyone did.

Going home crazy wouldn't help Beth very much, would it?

No, he told himself, it certainly wouldn't.

So maybe it would just be better for everyone concerned if he just found a comfortable chair and waited until things out there were under control. At least until the National Guard finally showed up and started covering the bodies.

And Marty was tired, so very, very tired. Every tendon and sinew in his body ached. He could feel the sting and pain of every scratch, bruise, gash, and bullet wound. His feet were swollen, scored with blisters. And he reeked of piss, blood, coconut oil, sweat, and drying mud.

Would he really be any good to Beth returning home like this?

He couldn't go on, not tonight.

Maybe not even tomorrow.

What he needed was a rest. A long one. Marty started looking for a place to sit.

The leather chair in the office wasn't bad, one of those big, over-stuffed executive models. It offered status, class, and absolutely no lumbar support, but it was perfect for what Marty had in mind. He was just about to try it out when he heard the whistling.

It wasn't really a tune, more of an aimless, semi-musical improv, the sound people make when the body is at work and the mind is on hold.

Marty followed the whistling down one corridor and through another. As he got closer to the sound, he also began to smell smoke.

The corridor curved and led him to an enormous, wood-paneled conference room. The long table was covered with stacks of files and computer disks, which a balding man, still in his Versace suit, was feeding into a fire he had going in a custodian's metal garbage can.

"If you've come to file a claim, we're closed," the man spoke without looking up, startling Marty, who didn't know he'd even been seen.

"Do you work here?" It's not that Marty really cared, but he wasn't leaving for a while and he wanted to know who he was stuck here with.

"I'm Sheldon Lemp, the CEO of Quantum Insurance. And if you have a claim, you'll have to come back another time, though we won't be able to help you then, either."

"I just want to stay here for a little while, if that's okay. It's safer than being on the street right now."

"You're right about that," Lemp dropped diskettes into the fire by the armful. "This building is made of solid steel with a spring-and-roller suspension system that allows it to ride out a quake. Most homes, by comparison, are made of wood and concrete which, no matter how much they are reinforced, will just crumble. Eighty percent of the properties we insure are homes."

"I thought most insurance companies got out of offering earthquake coverage after Northridge."

"They did, so people flocked to us, checkbooks wide open," Lemp lifted an entire stack of files in his hands and dropped them into the fire. Sparks flew out, forcing him to step back.

"Hey, take it easy," Marty said. "Those sparks could set the whole building on fire."

"It's okay, we're insured." Lemp laughed with delight bordering on hysteria. Marty watched him warily, trying to judge if the man was a danger to him.

When Lemp's laughter finally ebbed, along with the flames, he dumped more files into the fire. "This quake wasn't supposed to happen for another twenty or thirty years. That's what all the experts said. Did you know that?"

"No, I didn't."

"Since 1994, we've written 17,000 residential earthquake policies in Southern California with an average annual premium of $1400. That generated an enormous amount of cash, which I invested to capitalize our reserves and maximize profits. Since I'd been assured there wouldn't be another quake for decades, I felt comfortable with a greater level of risk than our board of directors did, so I found inventive ways to circumvent their oversight."

"I see," Marty glanced again at the hundreds of files and disks that covered the long table. "You made some bad investments and now you don't have the money to pay your claims."

"There will be some legal issues to contend with," Lemp flung disks into the fire one-by-one, like little Frisbees. "Thousands of civil suits, certainly, as well as criminal prosecution on state and federal charges."

"So you're destroying the evidence."

Lemp laughed again, an anxious twitter. "Oh, there's far too much of that. I can only hope to hide one, negligible aspect of my financial activities, some modest loans I granted myself as token compensation for the valuable, additional services I was rendering for the company."

"Doesn't telling me all about it kind of defeat the purpose of covering up the crime?"

"Not really," Lemp smiled at Marty. "When I'm finished burning all this, I'm going to kill myself."

Marty wondered how long you had to talk to someone before their death had any emotional impact on you or whether just seeing someone before they died was enough.

He checked his watch. His eyes were so tired, he had a hard time focusing on the dial underneath the cracked crystal. It was nearly 8 p.m.

"Look, Sheldon, I'm going to find a couch and lie down," Marty said. "Could you do me a favor? Try not to set the place on fire before you off yourself."

"Sweet dreams," Lemp chucked a hard-drive into the fire and started whistling again.

Marty left the conference room and went back to the front lobby, which had three nice couches to chose from. Lemp may have squandered the company's cash, but at least he bought some good, comfortable furniture before it was gone.

He stripped off his pack, letting his wet, crusty jacket slide off his shoulders with it, then kicked off his shoes. His socks were stuck to his feet like a second layer of skin. Marty sat on the edge of the couch and carefully peeled them off, placed them on the coffee table to dry, and then he lay back, letting his body sink into the soft cushions.

Marty was asleep before he even closed his eyes.

CHAPTER NINE
The Morning After

T he building was ablaze and they were trapped on the top floor, cornered by the flames below.

"What are we going to do?" Fred Astaire asked him.

Marty handed him a rope. "Tie yourself to the pillar, we're going to blow the water tanks on the roof."

"We could all drown."

"You ever heard of anybody drowning in an office building?" Marty gave him a reassuring pat on the shoulder. "Trust me. I'll get us out of this."

Marty did a quick pass through the room, checking on everybody, making sure they were securely tied in place. Once he was certain everyone was ready, he strapped himself to a pillar alongside Paul Newman.

"You're the bravest sonofabitch I've ever met," Paul said.

"I'm just an ordinary man in an extraordinary situation."

"We got a word for that," Paul looked him right in the eye and morphed into Buck. "We call 'em heroes."

"As soon as this is over, I want to see that napkin collection." Marty took out the remote control and pressed the switch, igniting the explosives.

The entire building shook and the roof caved in, spilling 50,000 gallons of water into the room, the torrent sweeping tables and chairs and people right out *the windows. He held on tight, the current raging against him. Suddenly, Marty's rope slipped free of the pillar and he felt himself tumbling across the floor towards the San Francisco skyline and a 90-story drop.*

"No!" he screamed, the water carrying him out into the night sky, sending him plummeting in cartwheels to the ground.

Suddenly the piss blankets around him pulled taut, and he was dangling in daylight just a few feet over the doomed 747, stewardess Karen Black staring up at him through the gaping, ragged gash in the cockpit. Her eyes told Marty everything, told him of her desperation, her fear, her need for him. Without him, they had no hope.

Marty looked up, following the string of piss-blankets back to the Army helicopter that was maneuvering him towards the pilotless airliner. He motioned to them to bring him down even closer, until Karen was able to grab him by his belt and guide him inside the plane.

As soon as his feet touched the cockpit floor, he grabbed hold of the pilot's seat to steady himself and released his urine-soaked lifeline. The helicopter immediately veered off to watch the drama unfold from a safe distance.

"Thank God you're here," Karen clutched him like a long-lost lover which, he realized, he probably was. "There's nobody flying the plane."

"There is now," Marty gently pulled himself away from her as her uniform transformed into a one-piece bathing suit. The old lady smelled of coconut oil and held a roll of toilet paper out to him.

"Don't worry," he said. "I'll bring this baby down safely."

Marty settled into the pilot's seat, only now it had become the driver's seat of a pick-up truck. He confidently took the steering wheel in his hands, wrenching it hard to the left, barely missing the fireball that shot out of the La Brea tar pit.

The pick-up truck skidded across Wilshire Boulevard, another fireball blasting the asphalt away in front of him. He wrenched the wheel again, the truck nearly rolling over as he skillfully avoided a streaking ball of molten death.

"Hold on," Marty yelled to Anne Heche, the beautiful, headstrong, presently heterosexual geologist beside him. He brought the car to a skidding stop. "Get out!"

They dived out of the truck just as a fireball slammed into it, blasting it to bits.

"Run!" Marty took Anne's hand and together they ran through the rain of fire spilling from the geyser of lava that towered over the LA County Museum.

At last, they were outside the reach of the molten spray, safely shielded by a tall building. He squeezed her hand and turned to her. "We made it."

Only Anne was gone. He was holding her dismembered arm.

Marty dropped it, screaming, and looked back the way he came. And then he saw Molly, trapped in her Volvo, slowly being consumed by the hellfire, her eyes pleading with him...

The sound of the gunshot shattered the image like glass and Marty bolted upright on the couch, eyes wide open, disoriented, frightened, his heart pounding.

Marty was in the lobby of an office. A breeze, and shafts of sunlight, came in through the blown out windows on the eastern side of the floor.

Then it all came back to him.

Where he was. What had happened.

Scattered memories of the nightmare, both the real one of the day before and the imagined one of his slumber, drifted across his mind.

Marty looked at his watch. It was 6:50 Wednesday morning. His mouth was dry, his lips chapped. His skin itched under clothes as stiff as cardboard. His ankle throbbed in the same spot where it fractured in the second grade. Even so, Marty felt a lot better than he did last night.

He reached down to unzip his pack and winced in pain. It felt like he was snapping muscles instead of stretching them, as if he was waking from the dead and discovering his body frozen by rigor mortis. He found a bottle of Evian, cracked it open, and drank it hungrily, letting the extra water spill over his lips and down his cheeks. He was tipping his head back for that last, glorious drop of water when his gaze fell on the chair across from him.

Marty gasped, choking on the water, coughing and gagging as he stared in horrified disbelief at what was sitting there.

Buck was slumped in the chair, his stiff body completely caked in dried mud and flecks of broken glass. The bounty hunter had clawed his way out of the grave to haunt him.

This wasn't possible. It had to be a mirage.

Marty picked up the empty Evian bottle and threw it at Buck. The bottle bounced off Buck's forehead and rolled across the floor.

Buck's eyes flashed open and Marty yelped again, startled.

"What the fuck's the matter with you?" Buck rasped, straightening up in the chair.

Marty stared at him. "Are you for real?"

"Did you just throw a fucking bottle at me?"

"It was empty," Marty stammered.

"Is that how you usually wake somebody up? You could show a little fucking consideration, especially after what I've been through."

Marty examined Buck closely. It was unbelievable. Impossible. Nobody could have survived that flood and found him.

"You're actually here, alive." Marty said, more as a question than a statement.

"You got a problem with that, Marv?"

"It's Marty. How many times do I have to tell you?"

"Whatever. Give me one of those frog waters. It feels like someone took a shit in my mouth."

Marty tossed him a water.

Buck caught it, twisted off the cap, and took a big swallow, gargling the water and spitting it out on the floor. He spit a few more times, then drank the rest of the bottle.

Buck stiffened, his eyes widening. "Oh, shit."

He abruptly leaned over and heaved a stream of vomit that would make Linda Blair proud. Marty scrambled out of the way, taking his pack with him. Buck kept heaving, his whole body spasming with each violent discharge.

When it finally stopped, Buck hunched over, exhausted, resting his elbows on his knees and letting his head sag down between his legs.

"Jesus," Buck muttered. "I must have swallowed the entire fucking stairwell."

"You were in the stairwell?" Marty asked.

"How the hell do you think I got in here?"

"I have no idea," Marty sat on the arm of the couch, looking at him. "It makes no sense to me. I saw you walk away. You weren't anywhere near me or this building."

"I doubled back and followed you."

"Why?"

"Because you're so goddamn helpless. I wanted to make sure you at least got to Cahuenga alive," Buck lifted his head. "I never thought you'd end up saving my ass."

"I didn't do anything," Marty said. "I didn't even see you."

"I was just standing there, staring at that fucking wave, when you bolted right past me. Snapped me out of a fucking trance. I ran after you into the building, but the water caught me just as I got to the stairwell. I couldn't see a fucking thing, I could barely move. It was like swimming through wet cement. Just when I thought I was gonna drown, I hit a railing, grabbed it, and started pulling myself through the shit, and I mean shit. I got out, crawled up a few steps, and fainted like a fairy. Woke up two hours later beside the fucking woman from Jaws."

Marty didn't want to think about the woman in the stairwell again. "Sounds to me like you saved yourself."

"I followed you," Buck said. "You led me into the stairwell, therefore you saved my life. Almost makes me sorry I shot you."

"You're forgiven."

"Fuck you. I said almost, asshole. You're lucky I don't have my gun or I'd be tempted to shoot you again."

"You lost it in the water?"

Buck jerked his head toward the hall. "I loaned it to dickhead."

Marty suddenly remembered the gunshot that woke him up and it all came together. "Jesus Christ, Buck! The guy was suicidal."

"I know."

"You knew?"

"Why the fuck do you think I loaned him the gun?"

Marty dropped his pack on the couch, slipped his bare feet into his crusty tennis shoes, and without bothering to tie them, headed down the corridor towards the conference room.

Buck groaned, got up, and lumbered slowly after him.

The conference room was empty. All that was left was a clean table and garbage can, its rim scorched, smoke still pouring from inside it.

Marty came out of the conference room, nearly colliding with Buck, and started moving through the hall, peering into every office.

"How could you give him your gun?" Marty asked.

"He was standing in front of a window but didn't have the guts to jump. The loser asked me to push him. There was no fucking way I was gonna do that, so I gave him my gun."

"Which office?"

"The big one in the corner."

Marty rushed down the hall. Buck trundled after him.

They found Sheldon Lemp sitting in the big, executive chair with the lousy lumbar support, the back of his head blown off. The mud-encrusted gun was still in his hand, his arm loosely hanging off the upholstered arm-rest.

"You could have just walked away, Buck," Marty said. "He might still be standing at that window if you had."

"Or not." Buck walked over to Lemp and examined the back of the chair. "Want to hear something funny? Guess what company insured my apartment?"

All the ugly ramifications hit Marty at once. This was getting worse with each second. "You're telling me you essentially murdered the man."

"No, I'm telling you why I essentially don't give a shit that he's essentially dead." Buck pried his gun out Lemp's hand.

"The police might have a different interpretation."

"You gonna tell them?"

Marty looked Buck in the eye. They both knew Marty wouldn't.

"This company insured your apartment. This guy squandered all their money. And he was shot with your gun," Marty said emphatically. "I think they can come up with a pretty convincing motive for murder all by themselves."

"Not without the gun, Columbo," Buck jammed it into his holster, "and not without the bullet, which went out the fucking window with most of his brain."

"What about physical evidence? A hair, a fiber, a fingerprint?"

"Oh yeah, right. Have you seen this fucking place?" Buck snorted, walking past him into the corridor. "Is there a kitchen around here?"

Marty took another look at Lemp. Buck was right, no one would care, not after the thousands who'd died in the quake and certainly not after they found out what Lemp had done.

And the truth was, Marty really didn't care either. He just wasn't used to people dying. But that was changing.

T hey gorged themselves on a breakfast of potato chips, granola bars, Oreo cookies, Pop Tarts, and five different flavors of warm Snapple.

It was the best meal Marty ever had.

Afterwards, Marty gathered up a bunch of bottled water, some more granola bars, and shoved them into his gym bag, then went looking for skin cream for his sunburned face and neck. He went through the secretaries' desks and discarded purses. Women always carried skin cream. His faith in female human nature was rewarded. He found some Neutrogena and took it with him to the bathroom.

It looked like someone had shot the place up with an Uzi. The floor was covered with shards of glass and tile which crunched under his feet. He stepped carefully, remembering that scene from Die Hard when Bruce Willis had to pull the broken glass from his bloody, bare feet. Marty was wearing tennis shoes, but he still wasn't taking any chances.

Marty glanced at the toilet stalls and wished he had the urge to crap. He didn't know when he'd come across a toilet and a latched door again. Even though there was no running water, Marty pissed in the urinal because that's what you're supposed to do, even if it wasn't working.

Buck felt no such obligation. Right after breakfast he pissed out the window and told Marty how wonderful it felt.

Marty zipped up his fly and went to the sink to apply his skin cream. When he looked at himself in the cracked mirror, he was startled by the face that stared back at him. The boyishness that had always characterized his face, that he had used to his advantage for so long, was completely gone. It wasn't the gash on his forehead, the dried blood and dirt in his hair, the sunburn, or the stubble that was responsible.

His blue eyes always had a sparkle, even when he was angry, and his face had a relaxed, easy charm that appeared to veil an incipient grin. But now his blue eyes were dulled, as if they'd darkened a shade, and there was a strange tautness to his skin, like setting clay. It scared him.

He didn't look like a network executive or a writer any more, that softness and sterility that comes from being kept fresh in cool, recirculated air under artificial light was gone. He was unkempt, and dirty, and a bit desperate, like a homeless person, but without the necessary aura of defeat and aimlessness. There was something else, something new and yet familiar.

Marty studied himself closer, his face not quite fitting together, cut into puzzle pieces by the cracked mirror. He recognized it now: it was the face of one of those perspiring submarine sailors in a war movie, waiting for the next depth charge to blow. The sailor feeling so many things all at once: Claustrophobia. Resignation. Fear. Bravery. Uncertainty.

Or was it something else? What was that expression? That look in the eye? Who was he now?

Oh, stop it! Your face is fine, he scolded himself. How can you judge yourself in a broken mirror? Anybody's reflection would look strange in dim light and broken glass. It's just fatigue and sunburn, nothing a little sleep and some cream won't cure. Don't worry about it. You're the same man you always were.

But as Marty rubbed the lotion into his face, he knew that wasn't true. Something was different.

Marty and Buck met in the lobby a few minutes later as Marty was pulling on his rigid socks.

"Good news," Buck said. "There's a fire hose on the floor. I bet every floor has one."

"So?"

"We're going to need it to get out of here."

"I don't follow."

"Because you aren't half as smart as I am. Ask yourself how we're gonna get out of here."

"The same way we came in," replied Marty, though he dreaded the prospect.

"The stairwell and lobby are gonna be stuffed with cars, trees, houses, who knows what-the-fuck else. Even if we could climb through it, all that shit has got to be unstable. So we're gonna go down to the first floor, tie a fire hose off to something solid, and lower ourselves out. *Comprendo?*"

Marty nodded, tying his shoes. "*Comprendo.*"

"So where we going after that?"

"We?"

"Are you fucking brain dead or just an asshole?" Buck let his eyes bore into him.

Obviously, Buck had no place to go to, and no one waiting for him, and was too proud a man to admit he was lonely or afraid. Marty knew that, but his compassion couldn't seem to get past his innate dislike of the man. Why couldn't Marty admit to himself that he was overjoyed that Buck was alive? That he was thankful he wouldn't have to make the journey alone?

"An asshole," Marty conceded.

Buck just grunted, not the least bit mollified by Marty's admission.

"Here's my plan," Marty said. "We'll head south until we're away from the worst of the flood damage, then work our way back northwest and take the Sepulveda Pass into the valley."

Buck was still glaring at him. "What if you need some help lifting your house off your wife, did you think of that?"

"No, I didn't."

"Which means you're brain dead and an asshole." Buck walked off towards the stairwell.

Marty figured he deserved that. He put on the leather work gloves he stole from the grip truck, adjusted a dust mask over his nose and mouth, slipped his bulging gym bag on his back, and followed Buck into the stairwell.

8 :04 a.m. Wednesday
The repulsive stench of decay in the stairwell was unbearable, but it was a rose garden compared to the street, which they could smell even as they wriggled down the fire hose from the first floor.

Bodies, and pieces of bodies, were strewn everywhere. Not just men, women and children either, but dogs, cats, horses, even birds. The corpses were all enmeshed in mountainous, decomposing tangles of rotting food, electric wires, slabs of concrete, clothing, motorcycles, and bus benches, among all the other things, large and small, that make up a city.

Marty and Buck had to wade, and climb, and crawl over it all, while trying not to see, breathe, or touch any of it out of the natural fear that death was contagious.

The two men weren't alone on the streets. There were survivors rooting through the wreckage, desperately searching for lost loved ones, and the rescue workers helping them pick through the rubble, sharing their senseless hope for a miracle.

But Marty didn't look at those people. He concentrated on just moving forward, distracting himself from the overpowering smell and the grotesque mosaic of violent death by thinking of Beth, of the life he was returning to, the life they had before their world changed.

I know it doesn't make any sense. We're both married, and we both love our spouses. But you can't deny there's something powerful between us." Beth stood in front of him and took a step closer, moving into those few inches of space between two people reserved for lovers.

"I can," Marty read the words in the script, he didn't try acting them. He didn't know how. It was one of the many reasons he felt awkward helping Beth rehearse.

"Bullshit," Beth said. "Look into my eyes and tell me you don't want to kiss me."

"I don't want to kiss you."

She took another step closer. "Tell me you don't want to hold me."

"I don't want to hold you."

She came even closer, their bodies nearly touching. "Then what do you want?"

Marty looked down at the pages in his hand, embarrassed that it was shaking, and read aloud: "Logan suddenly grabs her shirt and rips it open, buttons flying, and buries his face hungrily between her breasts in a lust-driven frenzy."

"Do it," she said huskily, staying in character.

"What?"

"Do it."

He dropped the script on the floor, grabbed the front of her shirt, and tried to rip it open, but the damn buttons wouldn't tear off. He yanked again. And again. Beth began to laugh, and so did Marty.

"What did you do," Marty asked, grinning, "weld these buttons on?"

"Weakling," she teased.

"Okay, Wonder Woman, you try it."

Beth pushed his hands away and tried to rip open her shirt herself. The buttons wouldn't tear for her either, which only made it funnier. Neither one of them could stop laughing.

"Maybe if I undid a couple buttons," she untucked her blouse and opened a few buttons at the top, revealing a hint of cleavage. "Try again."

Marty slipped his fingers between the buttons, made sure he was holding tight, and pulled as hard as he could. One, lousy button came off, the others held fast. The two of them erupted into laughter again, leaning against one another in a clumsy embrace.

"I bet Lorenzo Lamas isn't going to have a problem doing it," she said.

"Fuck him." Marty replied.

"I will," Beth smiled mischievously.

"Oh yeah?" Marty grabbed her by the front of her blouse and yanked, ripping it wide open. She drew his face to her breasts and kissed the top of his head, running her fingers through his hair.

"You're just like an actor, Marty. All you need is the right motivation."

CHAPTER TEN
Getting to Know You

10:20 a.m. Wednesday
Marty's feet were killing him. He'd been walking on blisters all morning, and it was only getting worse. It was hard enough working his way through rubble, but now slogging through the muck, each step was like pulling his feet out of a bucket of moist chewing gum.

Marty and Buck had worked their way south down Vine to Melrose Avenue, where the flood seemed to have lost most of its destructive force, and were taking the street west towards Beverly Hills. Melrose Avenue was a literal dividing line between poverty and wealth, the grime of Hollywood and the grace of Hancock Park. The north side of Melrose was lined with run-down apartments, car repair garages, pawn shops, and a Ralph's Supermarket that was surrounded by a white, wrought-iron fence and guarded by armed security personnel. Across the street, estate homes and elegant condominiums abutted the tip of the exclusive Wilshire Country Club Golf Course, hiding the perfect green grass from passing cars.

Those class differences were irrelevant now. Both sides of the street here were in ruins, the rich and the poor, identically swathed in blood and despair, huddled miserably together on the streets, the front lawns, and the parking lots, tending their wounds and waiting for the ground to stop shaking.

Over the last hour, several small aftershocks rippled through the ground, reminding Marty and everyone else the earth wasn't finished with them yet, widening cracks, toppling lopsided homes and slanted buildings, breaking what little glass hadn't broken yet.

It had been over twenty-four hours since the Big One, and in that time, Marty didn't feel he'd gone very far in distance and yet, at the same time, knew he'd traveled a long way from where he'd been before. It wasn't only his reflection in the shattered mirror that made him think that.

For one thing, Marty realized he was a stronger, more capable man than he ever thought he was. He'd rescued a child, survived a flood, and waded through an unspeakable landscape of death. He never would have imagined he could do one of those things, let alone all three. And, at the same time, Marty was ashamed to find depths of weakness and cowardice within himself he never suspected were there. He did nothing for Molly, leaving her to die, and would have done the same for Franklin, if Buck hadn't forced him into pulling off a rescue. Somehow, the cowardice wasn't nearly as unexpected as the heroism and endurance.

As much as Marty disliked Buck, he couldn't deny that somehow this one-dimensional TV character, this caveman in a polyester suit, had brought out the best in him even while trying to get him killed. Yet all Marty knew about Buck was that he was a bounty hunter, drove a Mercury Montego, lived alone with a pit-bull named Thor, decorated his bathroom with cocktail napkins, and disliked women with slanty breasts.

"Tell me something, Buck. Who are you?"

The question didn't throw Buck at all, he answered immediately, without hesitation: "Two hundred and twenty pounds of exquisite manhood, loved and worshipped by women, feared and respected by men, my towering intellect matched only by my gigantic cock. One look at me will tell you all of that."

"What do you get if you dig deeper?"

"You get to experience it, which is different for women than it is for men." Obviously, Buck had given this some thought. Perhaps now Marty would actually learn something.

"For a woman, it means no bullshit," Buck explained. "I give them exactly what they want, what a man was put here to give them: good food, a solid fuck, and protection from harm. Until I get bored and find myself another woman. But I don't give them any bullshit. When I'm done with a woman, she knows it and I walk away. They respect that, even if it hurts, which is why any woman I've left will always take me back to bed again. That, and the fact I've got a huge dick.

"Now for a guy, it depends whether you're friend or foe. To a friend, I'm a fellow warrior, someone you know will fight alongside you to the death. A brother in blood, through heaven or hell. What's mine is yours, and that includes my woman. To a foe, I'm pure, primal terror. I'm the big, dark, merciless motherfucker from hell who will catch you, slit you wide open, and feast on your steaming guts."

"Steaming guts." Marty shook his head.

"That's what I said."

"That's not a description of a real person, that's a comic book character."

"I'm standing here, aren't I?"

"That's not who you are, what you just told me is an idiotic soldier-of-fortune fantasy shared by legions of minimum wage, illiterate rednecks who regret being born too late to fight in Vietnam and think Chuck Norris is a terrific actor. It's not who you are."

"What the fuck do you know? You're some professional bullshit artist who spends his days watching other bullshit artists pretend to be other fucking people living other fucking lives, and you think you can tell them how to do it better because you're so goddamn good at living a fantasy yourself."

"Is that how you see me?"

"Isn't that how you see yourself?"

As a matter of fact, it was. "No," Marty replied.

Buck shrugged. "Okay, then who the fuck are you?"

"I'm just an average guy."

"That's it?"

"I left out the part about having a gigantic cock and eating my enemy's steaming guts, but other than that, yeah, that's it."

"How would you know if you're an average guy? What the hell is that? It's meaningless bullshit. C'mon, who the fuck are you?"

107

"I'm a writer. I'm a husband. I'm a decent man."

"Uh-huh," Buck was silent for a moment, mulling something over as they walked. "So, what have you written?"

Marty looked away, suddenly uncomfortable. "Some scripts, some novels."

"Any of 'em shot or published?"

"Not yet."

"Then you aren't a fucking writer," Buck said. "So, how's your marriage?"

"What do you mean?"

"I mean does your wife love you? Is she happy? Is she getting what she wants out of life by being with you? Are you fulfilling all your requirements as a man?"

Marty thought about his conversation with Beth in the kitchen yesterday morning. He thought about his infertility. He thought about the awkwardness, the buried resentments, and the pain. "It's not that easy. You can love someone and still have times where--"

"You're a lousy husband," Buck interrupted. "Let's move on to the decency part. What was your first instinct when that black kid on the overpass needed help?"

Marty didn't answer.

"So you're not a writer, not a husband, and not a decent guy," Buck said. "We're back where we started, aren't we, Marty? Who the fuck are you? You obviously aren't the guy you think you are. So, you tell me which one of us is full of shit."

Buck was right. If Marty expected an honest answer from Buck, he had to give one himself.

"Okay, Buck. Fair enough. I'll start again. I'm an average guy in that I have dreams that aren't fulfilled, a marriage that isn't perfect, and am often more of a disappointment to myself than I am to others. I'm not completely loyal or honest and I don't pretend to be the perfect friend or lover. I can be selfish, manipulative, and cruel, just like everybody else. But like most guys, I try to rise above my shortcomings, or at least convince myself that I do, so that most days I can think of myself as a decent person."

"Holy shit," Buck said. "That's good."

Marty gave him a nod. "Your turn."

Buck took a deep breath, thought for a moment, then said: "Maybe I'm a bounty hunter, and spend all my time chasing people, because I'm on the run myself. Afraid of commitment, love, actually investing myself in anything. It's why I come across so big and mean, so people will be scared off and I won't have to deal with them on any sort of emotional level. Bottom line, I'm terrified of intimacy."

Marty looked at Buck, truly astonished. There was a human being somewhere inside Buck after all, and a surprisingly perceptive one at that.

"You like it?" Buck asked.

"I may have misjudged you, Buck."

"Now all the things I've done that piss you off don't seem quite so bad, maybe even redeemable."

Redeemable? Since when did Buck use words like that?

"You see a side of me that's thoughtful, sensitive, what you might call likeable," Buck said. "Am I right?"

Marty stopped walking. *Redeemable? Likeable?* Buck wasn't talking about himself. He was talking about a *character.*

"Everything you just said about yourself was pure bullshit, wasn't it?" Marty said. "You don't believe a word of it."

"Why do I have to believe that whiny, self-serving horseshit if you buy it and it works for the character?"

"What character?"

"My character, asshole. The hero of the fucking series. By the way, you were right, you do give great notes."

"What are you talking about?"

"That speech you just made, the 'I'm an average guy' thing, fucking brilliant. The way you gave yourself notes on yourself, that was inspiring shit. I saw right then what you were looking for, so I reworked everything."

"Reworked what?"

"The character, the whole fucking series. I made it richer, right off the top of my head."

This is unreal, Marty thought. The hands-down winner for the nightmare pitch of all time. "Why does every conversation we have always end up being about you and a TV series? I'm not interested in doing a show about you. I never was and I never will be. Got it? *Comprendo?* Can we fucking move on?"

"You asked me, remember? You're the one who started the fucking conversation."

"I didn't ask you to pitch me a series about yourself."

"Then what were you asking me about?"

"You, Buck. I wanted to know about you."

"Why the fuck would you want to know that?"

"You're right," Marty replied. "My mistake."

Marty was about to start walking again when he saw a man in a white chef's apron sweeping broken glass and stucco outside a small, ivy-covered restaurant, the vines all that was holding the building together.

"Oh, shit," Marty whispered.

Buck followed his gaze. "What?"

"That's Jean-Marc Lofficier, the famous chef. He owns La Guerre, the restaurant over there. I can't believe I nearly walked right by it."

"You hungry already?"

"No. I can't let him see me like this. Let's go south one block, we can come back to Melrose later."

Buck stared at Marty, incredulous. "You're afraid of a cook? What's he gonna do, char your fucking cheeseburger?"

"You don't understand. That is one of the top five power restaurants in this city. It's where everybody at Paramount does lunch. If Jean-Marc sees me like this, I may never get a table there again."

"So fuck him, eat somewhere else. Look, there's a spaghetti place across the street."

"Someday, Buck, this mess is going to be cleaned up and we're all going to have to go back to work. As stupid as it sounds, in my business where you eat and where you sit when you eat is important. If Jean-Marc sees me like this, looking like I pissed my pants and swam through a cesspool, that's all he'll ever see anytime he hears my name. I'll never get a reservation. And if I can't get a table at La Guerre, I can't do business."

Buck looked back at Lofficier, who was bending over to hold his dustpan as he swept the trash into it.

"No problem," Buck said. "I'll introduce his face to my knee a few times and we can move on."

Marty grabbed Buck just as the bounty hunter was starting towards the chef. "I appreciate the offer, but I don't think a beating is necessary."

"If the guy is lying on the ground, choking on his teeth, he won't notice you walking by. Even if he does see you, so what? He'll look as bad as you, maybe worse."

"Let's just go down one street."

Buck reluctantly followed Marty into the fashionable, residential neighborhood south of Melrose.

"Philosophically," Buck said, "I've got a big fucking problem running from anybody."

"You're not, I am. And it's not exactly running. It's avoiding."

"I got a big fucking problem avoiding anybody."

They were walking past the entry-level residences of moneyed Hancock Park when Marty began to wonder if this was such a wise move. The houses on the tree-lined, leafy street were miniaturized versions of the grandiose estates several blocks south. These were homes for the almost-millionaires, the ones with teething kids, leased German cars, and nightmares about turning forty. This was where a lot of studio executives, producers, and directors lived.

What if one of them saw him? Every time he gave them a note, they would remember how he smelled today and snicker maliciously.

So Marty kept his eyes on the ground, just in case someone he knew was among the people seeking shelter in their Ranger Rovers or gathered on their perfectly manicured lawns with their requisite golden retrievers, eating lunch out of Laura Ashley picnic baskets they bought for evening concerts at the Hollywood Bowl.

Thinking of the Bowl reminded Marty that he did know someone who lived here, a friend in fact. He looked up in time to realize that, as fate would have it, he was just a few doors away from writer/producer Josh Redden's place.

Josh lived on McCadden in one of those little Spanish houses with the red tile roofs and white plaster walls. Marty had been there two years ago for party celebrating the second season premiere of *Manchine*. A short time after that, Marty and Beth were invited to the Hollywood Bowl with Josh and his wife, who had a box there. They sat through a couple hours of classical music, dining on Wolfgang Puck frozen pizzas and airplane wine.

Marty could turn around and run from Josh, but then he'd have to go back up to Melrose and take his chances with Jean-Marc.

There was also another issue. Did he really want to tell Buck they had to flee from somebody else?

Hell no.

So Marty weighed the pluses and minuses while pretending to stop and tie his shoe.

The way he figured it, he had some power over Josh, but none over Jean-Marc. There was little Josh could do to hurt Marty, even though he, unlike Jean-Marc, was in the TV business. But Jean-Marc could do more to damage Marty's status and influence with one unfavorable table seating or refused reservation than Josh could ever do.

So it was decided. He'd take his chances on running into Josh.

Better yet, rather than risk being seen, of being revealed, he'd take charge and seek Josh out and, by drawing attention to himself, control the situation and how he was perceived.

Yes, Marty decided, that was perfect. By not hiding, but confronting Josh, he seized the moment and shaped it, and its meaning, himself.

Besides, Josh was about his size, maybe the producer could loan Marty some fresh clothes so he wouldn't smell, and look, like a latrine any more. Marty would still arrive in Calabasas dirty, but not nearly as bad as he was now, reeking of transient piss, rotting food, and Hawaiian Tropic, among other things.

"Are you tying your shoe," Buck asked, "or fucking it? Let's go."

"I want to stop by and visit a friend. He lives around here," Marty rose to his feet, pleased with himself and his sound reasoning. "Did you ever watch *Manchine*?'"

"The show about the guy who was half man, half machine?"

"Yeah. My friend Josh wrote and produced it."

"I remember it," Buck said. "The guy was always sticking his finger into computers, blenders, telephones, and shit to make 'em work."

"That was his super power. He could meld mentally with any machine he touched and control it with his thoughts."

"Big fucking deal. I can do the same thing just by using the on-and-off switch."

Marty ignored the dig and studied the homes as they turned the corner and walked up McCadden. Most of the houses on the street were built in the late twenties and represented an eclectic mix of contrasting styles, from the turrets and balconies of French Norman architecture to the old-money formality, columns and brick of American Georgian.

Rather than detract from the stateliness of the neighborhood, inexplicably this mix only enhanced it. Such starkly contrasting styles would never be allowed where Marty lived. Architectural homogeneity was strictly enforced to maintain elegance and property values. Yet even now, with many of these homes decimated or badly damaged, the neighborhood somehow managed to keep its elegance and rarified air. Perhaps it had more to do with the impeccably trimmed hedges, unbelievably green lawns, and sparkling European cars.

The first thing Marty noticed about Josh's house was the "For Sale" sign in the front lawn. The sign was standing straight and undamaged, the house was not. It had tipped to one side, spilling its red tile roof and several walls onto the BMW in the driveway.

Josh and Nora were lying on chaise lounges beside a small tent and a bonfire pit they'd dug into their freshly-mowed lawn. All the personal belongings they'd salvaged were scattered around them in moving boxes and bulging suitcases.

Nora's left arm was in a blood-stained, make-shift sling and her face was a sickly pale. Marty couldn't remember whether she was a teacher or worked in an art gallery.

Josh's head was wrapped in a bloody gauze and his right eye was swollen shut. It also looked like he might have broken his nose. Something must have fallen on his head in the quake, but Josh seemed alert, even if he hadn't noticed Marty and Buck standing in front of him yet.

"I'm so relieved to see the two of you are okay," Marty said as he approached. Josh and Nora looked up at him, clearly not recognizing him. "It's me, Martin Slack."

They still stared at him. They seemed confused.

"Don't feel bad if you have trouble recognizing me, I barely recognize myself," Marty laughed awkwardly, the joviality entirely forced. "This is my friend, Buck."

They looked through Buck as if he wasn't there, and turned their attention back to Marty, clearly accepting who he was and that he was, indeed, standing there.

"What are you doing here, Marty?" Josh asked.

The producer didn't seem nearly as enthused as Marty expected him to be, and it threw him.

"I was worried about you," Marty replied.

Josh shared a look with his wife, then turned back to Marty. "When, exactly, did you start worrying?"

"I was walking by just now, and I remembered you lived here, and thought I should check up on you, make sure you're okay."

"Now you're concerned," Nora said pointedly. "How nice."

"We're fine, Marty," Josh sighed. "Thanks for stopping by. Say hello to Beth for us."

"I was hoping you could do me a small favor. I was downtown when the quake hit so I've got to walk home. To Calabasas. As you can see, I've been already been through a lot."

"You want to borrow the car?" Nora nodded toward the driveway. "Be our guest."

"Actually, all I really need is a fresh shirt and a clean pair of pants." Marty would have asked for some shoes, too, but he could see Josh's feet were smaller than his.

Josh scratched at a fleck of dried blood on his cheek. "What you're saying, basically, is you'd like the shirt off my back."

"Any shirt will do," Marty forced a smile, assuming Josh was making joke. Or at least hoping he was. "I just don't want to go home looking like this. I smell like someone pissed on me."

"Good," Josh leaned forward now, his face reddening with anger. "Now you know how I've felt every day for the last two years, you son-of-a-bitch."

That took Marty by surprise, and Buck loved it, a big grin on his face.

"What did I ever do to you?" Marty asked Josh.

"Nothing, Marty. Absolutely nothing."

"I thought we were friends."

"Bullshit. I thought we were friends. But I was wrong. As soon as *Manchine* was canceled, I never heard from you again."

"You know how it is," Marty said, "you get busy. I got a lot of shows in production."

"And did you recommend your friend Josh for any of them? Did you ever invite your friend Josh in to pitch pilots? Did you ever return a single call from your friend Josh?"

Marty didn't know what to say because the answers to Josh's questions were obvious. It was like challenging the existence of gravity. Josh was challenging the natural laws of the television business.

It wasn't personal. But once a show is canceled, the talent on it are tainted with failure, at least for a while. Marty would look foolish arguing that the producer of a flop show last year was the perfect guy to run a new show this season. Who's going to get excited about that? As far as returning calls and having lunch goes, Marty's obligation was to the guys with shows on-the-air. That meant that people without shows got put off indefinitely. Friendship didn't figure in to it.

But it had been a long time since Josh took an unwanted hiatus. Maybe he'd forgotten what it was like.

"You know how it is," Marty said, as sympathetically as he could. "You'd just come off a couple years on a marginally-rated show. We needed a breather. I'm sure you did, too. But you never stopped being my friend."

"Two years, Marty. That's how long I haven't worked. Why do you think I'm selling my house? In another month, I would have been living in this tent anyway. Thanks to you. And now you want the shirt off my back, too?"

"It's not me you're mad at," Marty said, "it's the business."

"We used to talk on the phone every day. We ate lunch together. You've been to my home. We've gone to concerts together. And as soon as my show is canceled, you don't want to hear from me any more. That's not the business, Marty. That's you."

"Boo-fucking-hoo," Buck snorted. "What kind of pussy are you? Your show sucked, so you suck. End of story." Buck elbowed Marty hard in the side. "Can we fucking go now?"

"Yeah," Marty said, then turned to Josh. "I'm sorry things haven't worked out for you."

"No you're not," Josh settled back into his chaise lounge. "Because every writer who fails makes you feel better about being a failure yourself."

It was exactly that kind of on-the-nose, preachy dialogue that made Josh's writing so flat. Now Marty felt justified not returning his calls. That, and the fact that what Josh said was absolutely true.

"See you around," Marty walked away.

They were mid-way up the block, nearly back to Melrose, when Buck spoke up.

"So that loser was one of your fucking friends."

"Yep," Marty replied.

"What the hell are your enemies like?"

Marty was beginning to wonder if there was really any difference.

CHAPTER ELEVEN
The Doctors

11:12 a.m. Wednesday

West of La Brea, Melrose became the self-consciously funky fashion center of Los Angeles before morphing, just as self-consciously, into the high-end, home decorating district as the avenue crossed San Vicente.

Marty and Buck were in the heart of the funky stretch, where stores with names like Wasteland, Armageddon, No Problem, Devastation, and Redemption competed in Marty's mind as the Most Tragically Symbolic.

But the greatest accomplishment of these fashion-sellers wasn't their prescience at picking business names but their skillful repackaging of thrift store hand-me-downs and garage sale castoffs. They discovered you could slap the word vintage on a ratty t-shirt, a rusted refrigerator, a dented Pontiac, or an old pair of reading glasses and suddenly it wasn't an out-dated, beat-up, broken piece of crap; it was stylish. It was hot. It was cutting edge. Vintage clothes, vintage furniture, vintage records, vintage jewelry, vintage cars, even vintage food, in the guise of a fifties burger stand, could all be found here.

Vintage stuff wasn't all that was hot on Melrose. Marty was surprised to see that an upscale porn emporium, selling ointments, videos, vibrators, chains, condoms, handcuffs, inflatable women, and anything else that might come handy in the bedroom, was doing a brisk business.

Obviously, no earthquake kit would be complete without a couple dildos.

Buck stopped to look at two mannequins, still standing in the shattered window of a clothing store that once offered "Goth Babe ensembles" and "butt pirate duds." The female mannequin was dressed in an Edwardian dress with a seatbelt corset. The male mannequin wore a crushed velvet pirate shirt and leopard-print tuxedo jacket.

"What kind of fucking freak wears that shit?" Buck asked.

But Marty was more interested in the store next door, which sold old jeans, old shirts, and new Doc Martens—heavy, no-bullshit shoes that would be perfect for a post-quake journey over buckled asphalt. And a clean shirt, no matter how many people had worn it before, looked pretty good to him right now, too.

Marty stepped through the broken window into the store, wading through the piles of clothes on the floor.

"What are you looking for?" Buck asked.

"Some clean clothes and a new pair of shoes. See if you can find a size twelve."

Buck drew his gun. "The hell I will."

Marty looked at him wearily. "What are you going to do, shoot me again?"

"It's what I do to looters."

"I'm not going to steal anything. I'll pay for it," Marty turned his back on Buck and sorted through some shirts, looking for a large. This was the third time Buck had pointed a gun at him and the impact had worn off. "I'll leave the money by the register with the price tags of whatever I take."

"You're stopping to go fucking shopping? What the fuck is the matter with you? I thought you were in a hurry to get home."

"I am, but my feet are covered in blisters, my shoes are shredded. I need new shoes if I'm gonna make it. And look at me. What do you think my wife is going to say when she sees me like this?"

"She won't give a shit how you look, she'll be glad you're

alive—or the bitch can fuck herself and we end this long walk right now."

"Fine, forget the clothes. But I need the shoes," Marty spotted something on the floor. "And socks."

Marty snatched up the socks, set a fallen chair straight, and sat down, yanking off his shoes. He could feel Buck's anger without even looking at him. "It's not about comfort, Buck. It's about necessity."

"Yeah, right."

Marty's socks peeled off his feet like a layer of dead skin. His feet were red and swollen, covered with burst blisters and festering new ones.

Buck picked up a pair of Doc Martens and tossed them at Marty's feet. "A hundred bucks, cash."

"I got the money." Marty carefully put on the fresh pair of socks, but pulling the fabric over his tender skin stung anyway. He slipped on the shoes and tied up the laces.

Marty stood up and walked a few steps. His feet were sore, but this was an improvement. The shoes were stiff, but in a good way. It was like having his feet encased in concrete. He could walk over anything now.

"You ought to try a pair, Buck."

He turned to Buck, and that's when he saw the reflection in the cracked mirror behind the bounty hunter, the reflection of a orange-haired guy stepping out of the back room, cradling a sawed-off shotgun.

Marty whirled around and discovered that having two barrels aimed at him instead of one definitely had an impact—especially when they were held in the shaky hands of a strung-out guy with a face intentionally skewered with a dozen drill bits.

"Hi," Marty said, his voice cracking. "Nice store you have here. It is your store, right?"

But the guy wasn't looking at him, he was staring over Marty's shoulder. Marty knew then, without even looking behind him, that Buck was aiming his gun, too, and that Marty was screwed front and back.

It was a scene out of a Hong Kong movie, repeated in a thousand inferior American homages, remakes, and rip-offs. The stand-off. Two men, standing eye-to-eye, gun-to-gun, the ultimate, obligatory showdown. Only there wasn't supposed to be an unarmed man standing between them. A woman maybe, preferably the buxom love interest of the hero, but not some terrified network executive quivering in his new pair of Doc Martens.

It was a delicate situation, and whatever Marty said next could very well mean life and death for all three of them. And Marty didn't want to die over a pair of shoes, so he would have to choose his words carefully.

Unfortunately, Buck spoke first.

"Hey, Ugly, seeing as how you're so into body piercing, you'd probably enjoy having a couple bullets shot into your face. So, if you don't drop the shotgun in three seconds, I'll do you a big favor and start shooting."

"Wait," Marty said. "No shooting. Okay? Everybody just relax. This is just a misunderstanding."

"You're wearing my merchandise, maggot, that's my understanding," the guy with the shotgun lisped. It wasn't easy speaking clearly with drill bits in his tongue and lips, and he wasn't trying very hard.

"I was going to pay," Marty tipped his head towards Buck. "Ask him."

"One," Buck said.

"Forget how he looks, Buck, he agrees with you," Marty yelled, now more afraid of Buck than the guy with the shotgun, who's arms were shaking even more. "He's only protecting what's his."

"Two . . ."

"Buck, no!"

"Three." Buck was about to shoot, when a woman's voice distracted him.

"If you want to spill blood, good for you," she said firmly, "Just don't waste it in here."

She was standing in the doorway to the street, wearing a Red Cross windbreaker and cap, her long, blond hair tied into a pony tail, her eyes hidden behind aviator sunglasses. Her hands were on her hips, her stance radiating her disapproval and disgust with the three of them.

"I got a couple hundred people who need blood and since you're so eager to lose yours, why not give it to me instead of the flies? Besides, we're giving out juice and cookies, and I don't see either of you providing refreshments."

Marty didn't wait for the two men to decide. He immediately

stepped aside, out of the narrow field of fire.

"Sounds good to me," Marty reached into his pocket for his wallet. "Let me just settle my bill first."

He put some money on the counter then turned back to the woman. "Lead the way."

She walked out and Marty followed, not waiting to see how, or if, Buck and Drillface resolved their standoff.

N oon, Wednesday

A few blocks west, the grounds of Fairfax High School had become a field hospital, with hundreds of patients laid out on stretchers, sprawled on the grass, or sitting on the pavement, either waiting to be seen or silently enduring their pain. At this point, only the most critically injured were receiving treatment, and they were inside the enormous tents. Helicopters constantly took off and landed, unloading fresh casualties and going off in search of more. It wasn't a war, and this wasn't an army encampment, but Marty couldn't get the theme from M*A*S*H out of his head anyway.

Marty was lying on a cot, watching the blood flow into a plastic bag from the tube in the soft depression of his elbow. There were other donors nearby—Drillface from the store, a Hasidic Jew muttering to himself in Hebrew, and an enormous, fat woman wearing all her finest jewelry, two rings to a finger, twenty necklaces around her throat. Marty assumed Buck was out there somewhere, giving a pint.

The Red Cross woman, Angie, had asked Marty lots of questions about his medical history, but she had to take his answers on faith before sticking him with the needle. With several hospitals destroyed, blood banks depleted, and thousands injured, Angie told him there was a critical need for blood and no time to test it for anything beyond its type. And they were getting to the point where they didn't even have time to do that.

Angie was forced to go out looking for anyone who was healthy enough to spare a pint of blood. She'd managed to recruit dozens of donors, but it wasn't nearly enough to fill the growing need. As soon as Marty, and the donors around him, finished giving their pint, she'd go out hunting for blood again.

She came over to Marty now and leaned down to check his blood bag. "How are you doing?"

"Fine."

Angie wasn't wearing a bra and he was ashamed of himself for noticing. He was on his way home to his wife in the aftermath of the worst natural disaster in history. Beth could be dead, or critically injured. What kind of guy would leer at a woman's breasts at a time like this?

Any guy.

Marty shifted his gaze to her face, hoping she didn't notice where it was before. "I never got a chance to thank you."

"For what?" she smiled.

Leaning over. "Saving my life. I could have gotten shot back there."

"It's what you deserve," Drillface lisped. "Scumbag."

Marty turned to him. "I paid for the damn shoes, and I would have paid for them whether you showed up with a shotgun or not." He looked at Angie again and lowered his voice. "You believe me, don't you?"

"No," she said. "And I don't care one way or the other."

"As long as you get my blood."

"Yep."

"Well, I'm still grateful to you."

"We're even." She gently brushed the hair away from the gash on his forehead and studied the wound. "That's a nasty cut. Were you unconscious for any period of time?"

"I think so. It's hard to say." Especially with her breasts in his face again. He tried to look somewhere else, but his eyeballs were caught by the tractor beam shooting out of her cleavage.

"Uh-huh," she reached over to a medical kit, poured something on a cotton ball, and dabbed at his cut. That broke the tractor beam.

"Ouch!" Marty squirmed. "Is that soaked with alcohol or bleach?"

"Sit still. Have you experienced any blurred or abnormal vision?"

"Yeah," he winced.

"Pussy," Buck said. "A real man would put a horsehair in the wound, cherish the sweet pain of infection, and wear the scar with pride."

Marty opened his eyes and saw Buck standing beside him, munching a handful of Oreos.

"I'm glad I'm not a real man," Marty replied. "I'll live longer."

Angie dabbed at his wound some more. "Is that what you were trying to prove back there? That you're a real man?"

"I just wanted to buy a new pair of shoes," Marty glanced back at Drillface, who sneered at him.

"And what about the guns?" she asked.

Marty glanced at Buck. "That wasn't my idea."

She leaned back, looking at him with concern. "Have you experienced dizziness, poor balance, or nausea?"

"Not in the last few minutes, but yeah, I have."

"I don't like the look of that laceration, or the bruising and swelling. I wish I'd examined it closer before, I wouldn't have taken your blood."

"It looks worse than it is," Marty said. "It didn't bleed that much."

Marty didn't mention the gunshot wound. His jacket was so torn and dirty, she must not have noticed the bloody rip in his shoulder. If he pointed it out, she'd probably tell the nearest police officer, and then he'd be stuck here for hours.

Besides, it's just a flesh wound, right?

"I'm going to clean that cut, stitch it up, then give you a tetanus shot. After that, you should stay put for a while."

"Eat my cookies and juice, I know."

"I meant until a doctor can take a look at you."

"I thought a doctor was."

"I'm a nurse practitioner."

Buck snorted. "A real man would crawl into an earthen shelter and apply a poultice of cow dung, bacon fat, and crushed leaves. Fuck this cotton ball shit."

"Ignore him," Marty told Angie.

"I think you may have a concussion," she gave him a grave look. As grave looks go, it was pretty good, but Marty still wasn't worried. He didn't know anything about medicine, but he was an experienced TV viewer.

"Mannix had thousands of them. All he did was rub the back of his neck and jump into his convertible. How serious could it be?"

"Nothing five Advil and a beer can't cure," Buck opined.

She sighed. Not just any sigh, but one that expressed her deep disapproval, frustration, and scorn. Women were particularly good at the sigh. Marty figured it must be genetic, that Neanderthal women sighed in exactly the same way as their mates returned to the cave.

"You really should wait and see a doctor," Angie said.

"I can't. I've got to get home."

"Where's that?"

"Calabasas."

"That's too far. You shouldn't be walking, not until you've had a neurological exam."

"And how many days until that happens?"

Angie didn't say anything, which told him all he needed to know. She sighed, a completely different sigh than the one before. This one signaled her reluctant acceptance. Marty motioned to the helicopter idling on the field.

"If you're so concerned about my health, how about having one of those choppers drop me off at home next time they pass over the valley?"

"Unfortunately, it's not a taxi service. I wish it was."

"Where would you go?"

"My mother lives in Marina del Rey. A condo two blocks from the beach. They say the ground under everything turned into quicksand."

"I'm sorry."

Angie shrugged. "I'm sure she's alive. I would feel it if she wasn't, know what I mean?"

Marty nodded, wanting to believe that was true, not only for her, but for himself.

Angie removed the needle in his arm, taped a cotton ball against the pin-prick, and told him she'd come back to take care of his forehead in a few minutes. She left Marty with a pack of Oreos and a small carton of orange juice.

Buck watched her go. "Did you see how she was trying not to look at me?"

"She was ignoring you. There's a difference." Marty wasn't in the mood for Buck right now.

"She wants a slice of the big pie."

"The what?"

"She needs the incredible Buck Fuck."

Marty couldn't believe Buck's insensitivity, not that he was Michael Bolton himself. "She hates you, that's why she was ignoring you."

"You don't know shit about romance," Buck hiked up his pants, ran a finger over his teeth, and wiped it on his shirt. "Stay here, I don't want you cramping my style."

As Buck marched off to offend Angie, Marty lay back on his cot and sipped some orange juice.

The cut on his forehead stung. He'd need stitches. The scar would give him character. And as he thought about it, Marty realized maybe Buck was right. He didn't know much about romance, not that the "incredible Buck Fuck" qualified.

Five years ago, Marty was still single and living as a freelance reader, taking a stack of scripts home each week to synopsize and critique for various studios. He was sitting in his apartment one day, reading a buddy-cop screenplay he was going to trash in his report—a script that would, two years later, become one of the highest grossing movies of all time—when his phone rang.

It was the UCLA Medical Center Emergency Room. Beth had been hit by a car in Westwood and gave his name as an emergency contact. They needed him to come down right away.

All at once, he experienced a string of clichés: his heart skipped a beat, his knees wobbled, and he had trouble breathing. Those feelings he expected. What surprised him was the terror. The idea that he nearly lost her, that she might be suffering right now, made him want to scream.

Marty demanded to know details, what kind of injuries she had, how badly she was hurt. But the nurse wouldn't answer his question; she just told him to come down as soon as possible.

He made the drive from their apartment in West LA up to Westwood in about fifteen minutes, running two red lights and nearly hitting a bike rider himself. Marty could barely see through his tears or think past his terror.

He was her emergency contact? He didn't know that. When did that happen? When did she decide to give him that responsibility for her? When did he become more important to her than her family?

Marty parked, wiped his eyes on his sleeve, and told himself to be strong. For her. He was her Emergency Contact.

Family Feud was on the TV in the ER waiting room as Marty rushed in. None of the worried people sitting in the stiff, plastic chairs were watching it. He knew his face looked just like theirs.

Marty went up to the desk, told them he was Beth's emergency contact, and they led him to one of the large rooms. Three gurneys were separated from one another by curtains. A little boy was sobbing, clutching his parents, as a doctor removed a nail from his foot. A woman in her twenties lay in a bed, covered with hives, reading People Magazine. And on the next gurney was Beth, her eyes closed, a big, open gash across her chin.

Her blouse was splashed with blood. Her legs, arms, and cheeks were covered with scratches. He swallowed a scream and rushed to her side, afraid to touch her.

"Beth?"

Her eyes opened and she smiled, grabbing his hand. "Oh, Marty, I'm so sorry."

"What are you apologizing for?"

"Scaring the shit out of you. I'm fine."

"It's okay," he said. "God, don't worry about it."

"I told them not to call you, but they insisted," she caught him staring at all the blood on her clothes. "It's nothing, Marty, really. It's from this cut on my chin. Nothing's broken, just a lot of scrapes and bruises."

Marty was so relieved, he thought he might start crying again. He willed himself not to. Emergency Contacts don't cry. They provide strength and reassurance.

"What happened?"

"I was crossing the street and this car came charging around the corner. You would have loved it, I dived out of the way like T. J. Hooker," she smiled again, which opened her chin wound like a second mouth. "Only T. J. would have gotten the guy's license number."

The cut on her chin was deep, right down to the bone, and still bleeding. His chin hurt just looking at it. He hurt everywhere she did and he wished that was enough to take the pain from her, to transfer it to him. If he could do that, he would.

"What do the doctors say?" Marty asked.

"They want to take a bunch of x-rays, just to be sure, and they want to stitch my chin. I don't know if they're listening to me, so promise me you won't let one of the interns sew me up. Get a plastic surgeon."

"Okay."

"Make sure it's a plastic surgeon. A scar could ruin my acting career."

If she was worried about that, she really was fine. "A little scar didn't hurt Harrison Ford."

"He's a man," she said, "it's different for them."

Marty smiled and squeezed her hand. He wanted to hug her, to let her know how full of love and relief he was right now.

"What are you smiling about?" she said, stifling a smile of her own.

"Nothing."

"I'm in pain here." She squeezed his hand back.

"I know."

"You're still smiling."

"Marry me."

The words came out of him with no warning, no thought. But when Marty heard himself say it, he didn't want to take it back or turn it into a joke. He knew it was right and that he meant it.

"What did you say?" she stared at him.

"I said marry me."

"I'm not going to die," she said, her lip trembling. "You don't have to do this."

"Yes, I do. I realize now I should have done it a long time ago. I've taken you and what you bring to my life for granted. I never will again."

Tears streamed out of her eyes, but not from the pain or fear. She smiled. "I suppose if the marriage doesn't work, I can always say I was under duress and on drugs when you asked."

"Is that a yes?"

She nodded. He leaned down, and as gently as he possibly could, kissed her.

A plastic surgeon did sew Beth up (and, years later, the scar was barely visible) and while she was being x-rayed, a nurse played on Marty's concern for Beth and got him to donate blood for accident victims not as lucky as his wife. In an odd way, giving blood made him feel a lot better, the same way it did now.

Lying on the cot, on the football field of Fairfax High School, a landscape of destruction between him and Beth, he almost felt as though he could touch her.

CHAPTER TWELVE
Swimming Pools, Movie Stars

12:32 p.m. Wednesday
Marty was anxious to leave and wasn't going to wait around to have his wound stitched up. He did his bit for the disaster relief effort and wanted to get moving before they tried to get him to do more. There was still the Santa Monica Mountains and a smog-choked valley between him and Beth.

He got up and looked for Buck, which meant he had to wander among the wounded with his eyes open and his head up, really seeing their faces for the first time. They were all the same. It didn't matter whether they were injured or not, or how seriously they were hurt. They all shared the same body language, the same expression. It wasn't terror, sorrow, or pain, though there was plenty of that, too. They all looked lost. Everything they were connected to was gone. Their homes, their jobs, their families, their own bodies, the ground beneath their feet, all shattered.

Marty remembered walking away from that collapsed overpass after rescuing Franklin. The first thing he noticed was Bob Baker's Marionette Theatre and he couldn't figure out how or why it existed. Back then, he didn't see the relevance of puppetry in a modern world. Now he did.

They were all puppets, animated by the properties, responsibilities, and relationships they were tied to, all the things that were missing now. The earthquake cut all those strings.

Marty knew he wasn't any different. He was grasping for that one string he had left, the one that led back to Beth.

And Buck, he was holding on to the one thin string that kept him alive: his tough-guy, bounty hunter persona. He needed to be a hero, to constantly prove his guts, to make a decisive move in a life-or-death situation, which was why he probably went out of his way to create those situations when fate didn't bother to.

At least that was Marty's instant pop-psychology take on things. It was probably simplistic and too easy, but it was the best explanation he'd come up with yet for Buck's impenetrable, one-dimensional personality.

He found Buck on a stretcher, giving blood, eating Oreos. It made Marty angry. Buck was the last person he expected to find lying around when they should be on the move.

"What are you doing? You already gave blood."

"Actually, I didn't. I was just eating their cookies."

Marty glanced at his watch. It was nearly 1 o'clock and he still had a long way to go. "Damn it, Buck. Why couldn't you have done this while I was doing it? Now it's going to take twice as long to get out of here and I want to get going."

"So go."

It wasn't a malicious retort. Buck said it casually, without malice or bitterness, taking Marty completely by surprise. Marty didn't know what to make of it.

"You mean it?"

"They need me here. Giving blood. Crowd control. Guarding the cookies. Whatever. I want to do my part. Maybe I'll even get one of those slick windbreakers."

Buck was trying to look at something, but Marty was in the way. Marty followed Buck's gaze, and saw Angie bending over a box of supplies, her back to them. It was a nice back.

"You really think you've got a chance with her?"

"Wrong question, kemosabe," Buck grinned. "What you should be asking is: how long can she control her natural urges?"

Marty couldn't recall anything Angie said or did that could have made Buck so hopeful. Maybe it didn't matter. Maybe she wasn't the real reason Buck wanted to stay. It came back to strings. He might have found his here.

Buck was always looking for opportunities to prove his heroism and his courage, and this one was ready-made. And best of all, there was a woman he could impress doing it. If Buck was really lucky, maybe he'd even get a chance to shoot someone.

"But if you need me," Buck said. "I'll yank this fucking needle out of my arm right now and we'll get the hell out of here."

Marty smiled. Everything Buck just said seemed to confirm Marty's conclusions about him. For the first time, he thought he really understood who Buck was.

"I think I'll be all right. They need all the help they can get here and, unlike you, I'm too selfish to stay."

"You got family responsibilities, Marty, that's not selfish. That's being a fucking man. I'll catch up to you later, make sure everything is okay."

"Any time, Buck." Much to Marty's surprise, he realized he actually meant it. "You know where I live. I'll leave your name with the guard at the gate, assuming there's still a guard and a gate."

Buck held out his hand to Marty. "We've been through battle together. That's a bond that can never be broken."

Marty shook it, put some real emotion into it this time. Somewhere back there, Buck became his friend and now they both acknowledged it.

"This is the third time we've said good-bye," Marty said. "I think we're getting better at it."

"Just try not to bring a big fucking wave down on me this time."

Marty smiled and walked away, marveling at how strange his life had become. He'd just invited the guy who shot him to stop by his house any time.

Wait until Beth hears about that, he thought.

And then, for the first time since the earthquake, he had a good, hearty laugh.

1 :00 p.m. Wednesday
Los Angeles wasn't so much a city as it was the undefined space between many small towns that had grown too close together. Unless there was an obvious cultural landmark, like the

Chinese Theatre or Rodeo Drive, it wasn't always easy to know where you actually were.

Marty didn't know when, exactly, he left Hollywood and entered West Hollywood. Had he been a few blocks north, on Santa Monica Boulevard, it would have been obvious.

From the east, West Hollywood began roughly where the Pussycat Theatre once stood. The theatre was still there, but around the time West Hollywood became a city, it transformed into the Tomcat, showing fare like I Love Foreskin, to better serve the community.

From the west, Doheny Drive was a definitive boundary line, with large signs on grassy plots on either end of the intersection informing travelers the instant they crossed into chic Beverly Hills or gay West Hollywood. The only thing missing was razor wire and a mine field.

But Marty was still heading west on Melrose, and indications weren't as obvious. He assumed he was in West Hollywood only because he wanted to be that much closer to home.

He still couldn't quite believe what had happened to him since he got out of bed. The most important thing on his mind that morning was Sally Sorenson's exuberant nipples and what he was going to say about them in a Standards & Practices meeting that afternoon. He had no idea that instead of talking about "excess nipplage," he'd be running down Gower Street, chased by 15 million tons of surging water.

Nothing in life, with the possible exception of disaster movies, prepared him for that, and in most ways, reality was stubbornly refusing to play by Irwin Allen's sensible rules.

Wasn't the day supposed to start with some wacky vignettes introducing him to the racially and morally diverse group of survivors he'd be stuck with?

Where were the doomed lovers, the conniving coward, the touching elderly couple, the idealistic fool, and the self-sacrificing innocent?

And shouldn't his sexy love interest be at his side and not off-camera?

He stopped to stare at the enormous Pacific Design Center, an eleven story, block-long slab of cobalt blue glass known by most Angelenos as The Blue Whale. Behind it was a newer, taller, bright green companion monolith, known by most Angelenos as The

Ugly Green Thing Behind The Blue Whale. To Marty they looked like huge, molded- plastic containers.

Just lift the lid and place people inside to preserve freshness!

Now both buildings looked as if they'd been dive-bombed by a squadron of architecture critics.

As Marty pondered the wreckage, another stark reminder of the immensity of the disaster he'd lived through, he wondered what his life would be like after this, how it would change him or if he was changed already. He was probably as irrevocably altered as the landscape around him. It was just too soon for him to know how extensive the damage was, or if it was really damage at all.

Marty started to walk away and immediately felt all that orange juice sloshing around inside him. So he stopped beside a pile of rubble, took a cursory glance around, opened his fly and pissed.

He was wondering why this didn't mortify him the way crapping in public would, and why men always found it necessary to piss against something, when an angry voice broke into his irrelevant thoughts.

"Cut!"

At first, Marty thought he imagined it, channeling the spirit of a very disgruntled Irwin Allen. You're doing this all wrong! Where's the microcosm of society? Where are Shelley Winters and Red Buttons?

But then the voice was back, louder and angrier this time. "Cut, God-damn it, CUT!"

Marty finished, zipped up his pants, and turned around to see a small, three-man film crew on the sidewalk across the street.

The obese camera operator lowered his 35mm Arriflex and spit out a gob of chewing tobacco, nearly hitting his lanky assistant, who was lugging the camera pack, totally lost in a daze that probably began with the first rumble of the quake a day ago. They struck Marty as a post-apocalyptic Skipper and Gilligan.

The director was marching across the street towards Marty, who immediately pegged the guy for the job because the only thing he was carrying was attitude and the cigarette between his lips. This would be the post-apocalyptic Thurston Howell, only downsized and edgier for the new millennium.

"Really, you were marvelous. Very special. Now do you think you could do the exact same thing, only without pissing this time?"

"What was I doing?"

"You were mankind," The director held up his hands in front of him, making the lower edges of a frame for himself with his index fingers and thumb. "I was panning down from the building and settling on your back, to give the destruction human scale, when you decided to whip out your schlong and piss."

"Now you have human scale and irony. You rarely find that in stock footage. You should be thanking me."

Based on the equipment Marty saw, and the subject matter, he figured they were shooting stock footage. It was Hollywood's oldest little secret. Virtually every movie and TV show ever made used some uncredited footage shot by others and already seen many times before. But it was the very innocuousness of the footage that made it possible to get away with it without most viewers ever noticing.

Marty started to go when the director suddenly blocked his path.

"Wait a minute," the director flicked away his cigarette stub and pointed to Marty's bag. "You work at the network, don't you?"

"No."

"How did you know I was shooting stock footage?"

Marty couldn't resist showing off. "A news crew would be using a video camera. You're using 35mm film, no sound equipment, no lighting, no real crew, and you're shooting a building and my back. It was an educated guess."

He tried to sidestep him, but the director blocked his path again, whipping out a card.

"I'm Kent Beaudine, King of Stock Footage."

Which is also what the card said, along with a drawing of a crown resting jauntily on top of a happy-faced film reel.

"You know the building in LA Law? That was mine," Kent said. "You ever see that shot of the full moon with a wispy cloud passing in front of it? Mine. Spielberg, Coppola, Scorcese, they've all used it."

"That's nice," Marty shouldered his way past him.

Kent motioned to his crew to stay put and fell into step beside him. "This is your lucky day."

"Doesn't feel like it to me."

"I know what you mean. Today we're witnessing a terrible tragedy and feeling the suffering of our fellow man."

Kent slowed, sidelined by all that suffering. He lowered his head somberly to ponder it all.

Marty slowed, too, despite himself, and looked at Kent. At that instant, the director looked up, his face alight with enthusiasm, and pointed his finger at Marty. "But tomorrow it's going to be a movie, we both know that. It's just a question of who makes it first!"

Marty groaned and continued on his way.

Kent hurried up beside him. "And whoever does is going to have to recreate all of this."

"The tragedy and human suffering."

"That's easy, it's the massive destruction that's hard. But you've got the inside track."

"I don't see how."

"No one has ever had good earthquake footage before. Everything's on video. It looks like shit, it never matches the rest of the movie. The audience knows right away it's fake, so you've got to spend a fortune on model work and CGI. Not anymore. I'm shooting this on 35-millimeter film. This will be the first, feature quality stock footage of a cataclysmic earthquake. It's going to be an evergreen. You'll be seeing this film in movies and TV shows for the next thirty years. But you, Marty, can be the first to use it."

Marty stopped. "How do you know my name?"

"It's on your business card," Kent tapped the laminated identification tag on the strap of Marty's bag. "It looks embossed. Very impressive. I've been thinking of doing that."

Marty suddenly had a notion, but it would take some investigation to see if it would work. "What kind of footage do you have?"

"Hollywood Boulevard submerged, the spires of the Chinese theatre poking through the mud. Geysers of fire shooting out of Farmer's Market. The La Brea Tar pits swallowing up Wilshire Boulevard. That's just for starters."

Marty suspected it might be his lucky day after all, but not for the reasons Kent thought. "You did all of that shooting in just one day on foot?"

"Hell no," Kent jerked his head towards his camera crew. "We used motorbikes."

Marty followed his gaze. There were three motorbikes parked on the sidewalk just outside the spitting distance of the tobacco-chewing cameraman.

Yes, indeed, it was Marty's lucky day. "Where are you going next?"

"I hear the Century City towers collapsed. Thousands of people died. It's gotta look spectacular."

"You ought to go to the valley."

"Yeah, right, like anyone cares. You've seen one pancaked apartment building, you've seen them all." Kent took out a pack of cigarettes, shook one out, and offered it to Marty, who declined.

The director stuck the cigarette in his mouth and lit it. "I'm trying to get landmarks, or what's left of them. That's what people what to see destroyed. That's what has emotional resonance and, more importantly, re-sellability. Why do you think asteroids in movies always hit the Chrysler Building or the Eiffel Tower?"

Kent took a deep drag and blew the smoke off to one side, away from Marty.

"You're right, of course." Marty said. "But I've got special needs. The movie I'm thinking about takes place in the valley and the city."

"You're thinking about a movie?"

"It's about a guy who's walking home from downtown LA to his family in the valley. The movie will shift between his wife and kids trying to survive in their ruined neighborhood and this guy's heroic struggle to get back home."

Kent thought about it a minute. "*Die Hard* meets *Cold Mountain*."

"More like The Odyssey meets Survivor. I see Tim Daly or Kevin Sorbo in the lead."

"I like it. It's fresh and original. I've never seen anything like it before."

"If you were to shoot exactly what I needed, it wouldn't be stock footage any more(it would be second unit work. You'd get a screen credit, maybe even a co-producer card."

"But I would still own all the rights to the footage in perpetuity."

"Absolutely."

Kent smiled and put his arm around Marty. "Let's go scout some locations."

1:30 p.m. Wednesday
Beverly Hills was not a city, it was a theme park. And today, the attractions, gift shops, and concession stands of Wealthy World were closed.

Marty shared a motorbike with Kent, holding the director loosely by the sides, as they snaked their way around millions of dollars in leased German cars left abandoned on the buckled asphalt of Santa Monica Boulevard. The Skipper and Gilligan, carrying the equipment, followed right behind them on the other two motorbikes.

They passed solemn, armed police officers leaning against their shiny, black-and-white Surburbans, manning the barricades that sealed off Beverly, Rodeo, and Camden drives from intruders.

And yet, just across the street, beyond the grassy park that ran alongside Santa Monica Boulevard, hundreds of Beverly Hills residents were trapped under their five-car garages, waiting for help that Marty knew would never come. The cops were too busy rescuing Polo shirts and dragging Cartier watches to safety from the flattened stores.

Those streets and the shops on them were the Smithsonian of Beverly Hills, where ancient history was measured in increments on a parking meter; where a Prada bag and an Hermes scarf were artifacts of incalculable cultural, artistic, and scientific value, at least until the new fall lines came in; where the original kinescope of the *I Love Lucy* pilot, screened hourly in the Museum of Television and Radio, was as well guarded as the Mona Lisa.

Kent made a U-turn, steered the motorbike onto the park across from Rodeo Drive, and stopped, much to Marty's annoyance. They had hardly covered any ground yet which, of course, was Marty's only reason for riding along with the stock footage crew.

"Why are we stopping?" Marty asked.

"Rodeo Drive is dust, we can't pass that up. It's like the fall of the Roman Empire!" Kent hopped off the bike and motioned the Skipper and Gilligan to park alongside.

Marty sighed, resigning himself to the inevitable. Even with the occasional stop for filming, he'd still move faster with Kent and his motorbike than without him. He sat down on the edge of a large, concrete fountain in the park to wait Kent out.

Kent looked at ruptured asphalt and crumpled storefronts of Rodeo Drive through the frame he created with his hands and yelled at the Skipper. "Get a couple wide angles from here."

The Skipper spit a gob of tobacco into the stagnant water in the fountain. "Without a crane, we aren't gonna see much from here 'cept the barricades. We gotta get closer. Those are the money shots."

"Just get the damn wide angle. I'll have a chat with the local constabulary." Kent took a deep drag on the small stub of cigarette he had left and exhaled slowly. "When I'm done sweet-talking them, they won't just welcome us onto Rodeo Drive, they'll help you carry the equipment."

While Kent sauntered across the street to work on the cops, Marty glanced at the fountain he was sitting on. It was a round pool about a foot deep, surrounding a cracked statue of a stout, naked nymph holding an armful of squirming, open-mouthed fish. According to the plaque at the base, the antiquity was a gift to Beverly Hills from Cannes, their official "sister city" in France. They'd probably been waiting 400 years for someone to unload it on.

The Skipper peered through the eyepiece of the camera, then set it down on the ground, abandoning the shot in a huff. "I don't see how I'm supposed to shoot anything with him standing there like that. He's right in middle of the shot."

Marty glanced back at Kent, who was waving his arms around, animatedly articulating a point to the stoic policemen. Kent didn't seem to be making much headway, which meant they could be here a while.

The thought made Marty look over at Kent's motorbike. The director had left the key in the ignition.

"You work at the network?" The Skipper asked Marty.

"Uh-huh." Marty's gaze hadn't left the motorbike.

"I worked a camera on *The Tortellis* in '87." The Skipper spit a gob of chaw and watched it arc through the air until it plunked into the fountain water. "Some people confuse that with *The Torkelsons* because they were both NBC sitcoms that started with a 'T.' But they weren't in the same league."

Marty nodded like he was listening when, in fact, all he wanted to do was jump on the motorbike and speed off. A couple things stopped him from acting on the impulse. For one, he'd never driven a motorbike. For another, it probably wasn't a bright idea to steal something in front of a camera and two police officers.

He shrugged off his pack and dropped it on the grass. Might as well get comfortable.

"*The Tortellis* was from the guys who did *Cheers.*" The Skipper spit at Gilligan, just to see if he'd jump out of the way. He didn't. The gob dribbled down Gilligan's shirt, but the dazed assistant didn't seem to notice. "It could have been *Frasier*, but it wasn't. It sure as hell wasn't *The Torkelsons*, though."

The Skipper jammed some more tobacco into his mouth and watched Kent argue with the cops. Marty watched, too.

From the irritated look on the cops' faces, it seemed if Kent tried to press his point any further, they'd gun him down. In a pique of anger, Kent flicked his cigarette stub at them and turned away.

The street exploded.

Marty toppled face-first into the fountain as a gale force wind of flame blasted through the cracked asphalt of Rodeo Drive and blew in all directions.

He felt the agony of the searing caress and heard the unearthly roar of the firestorm as it passed over him. His screams drowned in the water.

And then, only moments after it was ignited, the firestorm was gone, totally extinguished, absorbed into the air like a fine mist.

Marty immediately rolled over, his burning jacket hissing in the water. His back smoldered, red-hot needles of pain piercing deep into his flesh. He lay half-floating there for a long moment in shock, listening to the crackle of fire, astonished to be alive, trying to reconstruct what had just happened. He guessed that Kent's cigarette stub ignited gas that had accumulated under Rodeo Drive from a leak somewhere. The jolt of the blast knocked Marty off-balance into the fountain, and the ring of concrete and the foot of water saved him. The firestorm passed right over his back, scalding his flesh.

It felt like someone tried to iron his shirt while he was still wearing it. But it could be much worse. If it hadn't been for the two layers of wet clothing, he probably wouldn't have any skin left on his back at all. Marty sat up slowly, grimacing in pain, and looked around.

After all the destruction he'd already seen, he thought he was past being stunned by the epic scale of the devastation, by the familiar rendered into something altogether different and nightmarish.

He was wrong.

Beverly Hills was a blazing wasteland. Buildings and cars and trees were consumed by fire. Flames licked out of a huge crater where the pavement once was, feeding on the last wisps of trapped gas escaping from below.

There was no sign of the Suburbans, or the police officers who once leaned against them, or of Kent Beaudine, the casual wreaker of the city's doom. Marty assumed they were at the bottom of the crater, entombed with countless movie-star baubles.

The lavish houses and tall trees fronting the park were on fire, the ravenous flames jumping to the surrounding homes. It wouldn't be long before the whole neighborhood was burning. He'd have to move fast if he didn't want to get caught in it on his way home.

Wincing with pain, Marty lifted himself into a sitting position on the rim of the fountain, swung his legs over the edge, and was about to stand up when he froze. He'd nearly stepped on one of the smoking chunks of asphalt that covered the park like pieces of a meteor.

But that wasn't what made him stop in mid-motion.

The Skipper was lying on the ground, his body scorched naked by the fire, his skin black as charcoal. But he was alive, smoke curling from his nostrils, his lungs seared.

"I don't want to die," the Skipper squealed, looking at Marty with imploring eyes, smoke pouring out of his mouth.

Marty crouched beside him but couldn't bring himself to touch the man. "You won't."

But a few moments later, the cameraman did.

Marty didn't even know his name. All Marty knew about him was that he spit tobacco and worked on *The Torkelsons*.

It wasn't much of an epitaph.

He rose up slowly, unable to take his eyes off the horrifying sight of the dead man. Somewhere deep inside, the Skipper was still burning, thin wisps of smoke drifting out between his charred, dead lips.

Marty looked around for Gilligan and found him in pieces. The camera assistant had been decapitated by a piece of Rodeo Drive, his headless corpse slumped over the smoldering battery pack.

He looked away, repulsed and terrified. In a war, Marty thought, there must come a time when a person becomes inured to the carnage and violent death, when the experience changes from something unusual and shocking into something commonplace and expected.

That time hadn't come for him yet. He wished it would hurry up and get here or, if it didn't, that he could be spared any new variations on the theme. Marty didn't know how much more he could take.

His sanity felt almost physical, like a joint that had already been flexed too far. He knew it was about to snap, but unlike with a torn ligament or broken bone, he had no idea what consequences to expect if it happened.

Maybe it wouldn't be so bad.

Maybe it would be a pleasant numbness, a blissful separation from direct contact with reality.

Or maybe not.

It could mean losing all sense of self, all intelligence. He could end up a mewling idiot, staggering mindlessly through the rubble.

And then he would never get home.

Stop being a pussy. So people are dying horrible, grotesque, and painful deaths right in front of your eyes. Big fucking deal. Be glad it's not you and move on.

Lately, the voice in his head was sounding more and more like Buck and yet, strangely enough, seemed to be making more and more sense to him.

The way to deal with it, he decided, was to look at death clinically, the way a coroner does. When a coroner looks at a corpse—whether it's been hit by a train, torn apart by sharks, mutilated with an ax, mangled in a car crash, or left decaying in the sun for a week, infested by maggots—it doesn't sicken or terrify him. Why? Because it isn't a human being any more. It's an object, a by-product, a thing. A fleshy sack of organs and bones that just resembles a living thing.

Marty would just have to get in the right frame of mind.

But it occurred to him that coroners had an advantage he didn't. They rarely witnessed the killing, the moment when a person stops being a person and becomes a corpse.

Then again, millions of soldiers over tens of thousands of years had come to grips with that moment on the battlefield. And most of them didn't lose their minds. How hard could it be?

Be a fucking man.

Yes, Marty thought. That's exactly what I'll do. I'll be a fucking man.

He turned and faced north on what was left of Rodeo Drive. For the first few blocks, houses on both sides of the street were aflame and charred bodies were scattered on the sidewalks.

Be a fucking man.

Marty took one flap of his wet jacket, raised it in front of his face like a cape, and trudged across the blackened grass into the smoke.

CHAPTER THIRTEEN
Over the Hill and Through the Woods

2:42 p.m. Wednesday

The statues had pubic hair.

It wasn't some artist's chiseled interpretation of pubic hair, but actual hair of some kind glued to the carved crotches of a dozen stone nudes. Beyond that, the row of gaudy statues that lined the top of the wall around the Sunset Boulevard mansion would otherwise have been unremarkable.

When Martin Slack first saw those statues twenty years ago from the front seat of his over-heated Chevette, arriving from Northern California for his freshman year at UCLA, he knew for certain he'd arrived in Los Angeles.

The wall was still there, only now it was riddled with fresh cracks and surrounded an empty lot full of tall, dry weeds. The statues and the mansion were long gone, but they undoubtedly lived on in the photo albums of a thousand tourists.

The homeowners on Sunset wanted their properties photographed, not by Architectural Digest but by busloads of tourists, and would go to extreme, and expensive, lengths to get those snapshots taken.

The fervent competition for tourist eyeballs often made Sunset Boulevard look like a residential version of the Las Vegas Strip, only without the budget buffets.

To become a sidewalk attraction, it wasn't enough to have lavish architecture and lush landscaping, or to park shiny limousines and Italian sports cars around a sparkling fountain. Extravagance, opulence, and gratuitous displays of wealth were merely starting points.

Some homeowners made their blatant grab for snapshot glory only on the holidays, festooning their lawns and eaves with hundreds of flashing lights, elaborate floral displays, and animatronic dioramas that Walt Disney would have envied.

Others were in it for the long run, striving to become a permanent stop on the Hollywood Star Tour and yet, at the same time, maintaining the charade that they valued their own privacy with small "no trespassing" signs staked in their lawns.

One such homeowner decorated the circular drive in front of the white walls that sealed his property with incredibly life-like bronze statues—albeit clothed and presumably without pubic hair, real or otherwise. He began with only a uniformed security guard at his gate, then quickly expanded his repertory company of statuary to include a gardener, a painter, a jogger, kids at play, and in case anyone missed the subtle intention behind his efforts, a tourist couple taking pictures of it all.

Marty sat in front of this house, resting on the homeowner's sturdy, wood-carved "private property" sign. He didn't know or care if the house behind the walls still stood, the tall trees behind the wall hiding it from view. But he was glad the statues had survived because now, in his mind, nothing was more authentically LA than this.

Except, perhaps, for the statues with pubic hair, but sadly they were already lost. He thought somebody should have lobbied to give them protection as a historical landmark. They were significant to him, if no one else, even if he didn't really miss them until now.

Even though he'd traveled on Sunset countless times over the last twenty years, somehow this time it felt like he was retracing the path he took when he first came here from San Francisco, when he was full of dreams and plans that still hadn't come true.

His melancholy was compounded by his physical state. He'd never experienced so many different kinds of discomfort at once.

His back burned, his cuts stung, his shoulder throbbed, and his skin itched under his charred, damp, dirt-caked clothes. Every muscle in his body was sore, and his feet felt as if they had swelled to twice their normal size. He was hot, thirsty, and sweating all over.

And then there were all those dead faces that wouldn't stay buried in his mind, flashing in front of his consciousness like commercial breaks.

The memories, the weariness, and the pain became an almost palpable weight, carried all over his body. This must be why so many elderly people stooped, Marty thought. Seventy years of this shit must weight a lot.

So he'd stopped to rest, to clear his head, to marshal his strength for the next leg of his journey over the Sepulveda Pass. He knew the hills were ablaze, even from here he could see the smoke. But he was going to take the Pass anyway, because the alternative, trekking twenty or thirty more miles further west and inching into the valley from the coast, was unthinkable. It would take days in the condition he was in now and there was no telling what hazards he'd face there—mudslides, forest fires, deranged mountain lions, swarms of locusts.

The locusts seemed like a stretch, but then again, Marty never would have imagined running into a tidal wave in the middle of Hollywood, either.

He figured the Sepulveda Pass wasn't too big a risk anyway. He was planning on walking straight up the center of the San Diego Freeway. The ten lanes of concrete plus the two lanes of Sepulveda Boulevard should make a nice, wide fire break.

Marty took a deep breath, got to his feet, and started walking again. To distract himself from the pain, and to make the time pass, he sang TV themes to himself, beginning with fifties shows and moving forward from there.

He began with *Have Gun, Will Travel* and was up to *Green Acres* a half-hour later as he approached a guy near the ornate gates to Bel-Air, sitting in a lawn chair beside a sandwich board that advertised "Maps to the Stars' Homes (Only Five Dollars!)." The "five" had been scratched out and replaced with a hastily scrawled "two." The man was going through his maps, spreading them open on his lap and X-ing out homes with a fat magic marker.

"Doing much business?" Marty asked.

"Some," the man said, intent on his work. "News crews, mostly."

Made sense. It didn't matter much to Americans if Los Angeles was destroyed, Marty thought, but God save Jay Leno's garage, Brad Pitt's sun deck, and Meg Ryan's tennis courts.

"How do you know which homes have been destroyed?" Marty asked.

"I have my sources," he said mysteriously and started marking up another map.

Marty headed off again, picking up where he left off in the sixties with *Branded*. He was in middle of the seventies and *Good Times* when he passed the northern fringes of UCLA. The jogging track, like most open spaces he'd seen since the quake, was clogged with people in make-shift shelters and tents. Above them, to the west, the ruins of the dormitories lay across the stands like fallen stacks of Legos.

His first home in LA was gone. Scratch that one off the Martin Slack Historical tour.

Although there might be food and water on campus, he decided not to stop there for fear he'd never get started again. He walked on, reaching the San Diego Freeway just as he was entering the eighties with *Gimme a Break*.

The freeway stretched up into the hills, towards a pall of smoke a few miles north that blotted out the sun. The ten-lane roadway was riddled with fissures, ripples, and sinkholes and littered with mangled, wrecked, and overturned cars. The only traffic was a small handful of living dead, either heading into or out of the valley. Surprisingly, the people walking south stayed in the southbound lanes to the left, while those heading north remained on the right, as if those rules made any difference now.

Marty supposed they instinctively clung to the habit for the same reason he was singing TV themes. It grounded them, allowing them to forget what they'd seen, to move like zombies on a pre-destined course. So he headed north into the Pass and dutifully stayed to the right, belting out *The Greatest American Hero* with all the passion he could muster.

3 :25 p.m. Wednesday
After the Getty Center Drive exit, the hills on either side of the

freeway seemed uninhabited, except by flames, which swirled amidst the acres of dense, dry scrub-grass, sending plumes of dark smoke into the sky, turning day into night.

He'd read somewhere that an acre of brush was equal to 5000 gallons of gasoline. It didn't give him much comfort.

The fire had a sound, deep and heavy, like a waterfall only without the water. Glowing orange cinders swirled around him like red-hot snowflakes. Waterfalls without water. Snowflakes on fire. Walking through the Pass was surreal.

Marty's journey was getting much harder now, not so much the walking, but finding TV themes to sing. He was discovering that the eighties and nineties were mighty lean years for TV songwriting. That, and it was increasingly hard to concentrate on distraction with an orange-black curtain closing in on him from both sides.

He stayed low, and well to the middle of the roadway, snaking through the abandoned cars, trying not to look at the bodies and body parts also left behind. Instead, he struggled to remember the lyrics to *Helltown*. Sammy Davis, Jr. sang it, but Marty kept confusing it with the theme to *Baretta*, which was easy, since Sammy and Robert Blake did them both.

Little balls of fire rolled down the hillside and across the freeway like tears. He didn't know what to make of them until one rolled right in front of him.

Only it wasn't rolling. It was running.

It was a wild rabbit, a ball of flaming fur, fleeing from the inferno. The freeway was being over-run with burning wild life. And where these burning rats, squirrels, and rabbits perished on the hillside, new fires started. The blazing creatures, in death, were unwittingly increasing the size and ferocity of their pursuer.

At least on the freeway there was no dry brush to spark under their fiery corpses.

Just puddles of gasoline.

No sooner did the thought occur to him than one of the burning rodents ignited a puddle of fuel with a loud whoosh just a few yards away.

It burned out quickly, but it was enough to terrify him. Suddenly, in Marty's mind, those flaming animals became rolling grenades.

He hurried along, looking in all directions, trying to keep his eye

145

on every flaming creature, every drop of gasoline, every wrecked car, hoping to anticipate the next blast.

This was so damned unfair, he thought. After what happened in that downtown alley with Molly, and what he went through in Beverly Hills, he should be exempt from having to deal with explosions any more. Since Fate hadn't issued that exemption yet, this had to be another cosmic payback, retribution for demanding more explosions in the action shows on his network, despite the creative and financial pleas from the producers.

Blow something up, he'd say. Something big. You can never have too many explosions.

Now he was learning first hand how wrong he was.

To his right, a Jetta exploded, spinning through the air towards him like a gigantic sheet metal football.

Marty ran like a wide receiver, only he was screaming and this was one pass he didn't want to receive.

The car smashed into the freeway not far from where he had stood, cartwheeling over the top of several cars, then crashing into the low concrete median.

He stared at the wreckage in amazement, gasping for breath.

A rat did that, he thought. One hot rat.

Marty hurried on, frightened, performing "The Eyes of a Ranger" as loud as he could, the flames dancing along with him on the hillside like insane orange ghosts.

Up ahead, a deer stood shivering between two cars, staring at Marty. The animal was seared black, her hairless skin smoldering. Marty passed close enough to touch the deer, but didn't. "I'll Be There for You," he sang, turning away.

Marty marched on through *Mad About You, The Nanny,"* and *Baywatch*. By the time he got to *Touched by an Angel*, the sound of explosions was receding behind him and sunlight began to break through the smoke ahead, revealing the ruins of the Skirball Jewish Cultural Center and the two overpasses that crossed the freeway at its peak.

The smaller overpass, the one nearest to him, joined Sepulveda to a small street leading up to Mulholland on the other side. The span seemed intact, but Marty ran under it with a shiver of panic anyway.

The taller overpass ahead was massive, rising up several hundred feet to stretch Mulholland over the San Diego Freeway.

The span had collapsed on either end, creating a towering, concrete island out of the center section that remained. Marty could see maybe a dozen commuters stranded up there with their cars, castaways in middle of an urban ocean. From their lonely vantage point, the destruction in the LA basin and the San Fernando Valley lapped up against their concrete pillars like waves.

The choppers heading into the valley must have seen them up there, which could only mean the castaways were a low priority compared to the calamities elsewhere. That must have been little comfort to them, especially as each new aftershock shook them like glassware on a wobbly table.

The castaways looked down at him sadly as he passed.

"Help us," a woman whimpered, her voice echoing off the roadway.

He looked up at her. There was nothing he could do, and saying so wouldn't make a difference. So he just lowered his gaze and continued on.

Once again, Marty had little choice but to go under the unstable span, passing the piles of cars, concrete, and rebar that had come down in the quake. A man's unscratched arm stuck straight out from amidst the rubble, coated with a fine layer of dust, a cell phone still clutched in his hand. For a moment, Marty thought about taking it and trying to place another call to his wife, but he couldn't bring himself to do it.

Buck would have, if he had anybody to call. Marty wondered who that made the better man.

Marty emerged from under the overpass and the valley opened up below him. He could see clear across to the San Gabriel Mountains on the other side. And in the concrete, sub-divided flatlands in between, through the haze of smoke, the face of the Big One stared back at him.

It was an angry, wickedly malicious face, the face of a vengeful giant who awakened from a deep sleep and dribbled a gigantic basketball up and down the valley, gleefully smashing entire blocks with each bounce.

Now the giant had taken his toys and crawled back into his hole in the ground to hibernate for a hundred more years before wreaking havoc again. By then, the mess would be cleaned up and everything rebuilt for him to destroy again.

Marty couldn't see Calabasas from here, it was ten miles east, but he imagined it hadn't fared much better.

He set off down the hill towards home.

4

:07 p.m. Wednesday

Los Angeles shouldn't exist. It had no natural harbor, no dependable water supply, and bad air. All it had going for it was year-round sunshine.

That was more than enough, with the right spin.

Nothing symbolized this more than the San Fernando Valley, once a parched dust bowl baking under the incessant heat.

But Los Angeles Times publisher Harrison Gray Otis and a few other wealthy businessmen saw the potential under all that cracked, dry earth. It was lousy farmland but these businessmen were interested in harvesting a more resilient crop: money. But to do it, they'd still need water.

Otis and his cronies bought up all the struggling farms and only then used their considerable clout to divert water along massive aqueducts from the Sacramento Delta hundreds of miles north to the arid valley.

With the arrival of water, the land was worth hundreds of times what the businessmen paid for it. And what they didn't own, they took control of by annexing it into the city. Otis used the pages of his newspaper to hype the valley as paradise and soon the people came in hordes.

Of course, Marty wouldn't have known any of this if he hadn't seen Chinatown. And if he hadn't seen the movie, and learned about the scandal and dirty-dealing behind the valley's creation, he couldn't have lived there. Without a hint of scandal in its past, the valley would have been just too bland to be habitable.

The only natural source of water to the valley was the Los Angeles River, which remained bone dry half the year, only to swell in the winter as much as three-thousand fold in a single rainy day. As much as Los Angeles craved water, it didn't appreciate the unpredictability of the river and treated it as they would any other piece of land. They paved it.

Now the Los Angeles River was a concrete-lined flood channel that snaked through the valley, except for one small patch designated as a park, where the Streamline Moderne-style Sepulveda Flood Control Dam held back the water when necessary and served as a cheap film location the rest of the time.

Even when the river was flooding, there was no shortage of exciting film to be shot. Inevitably, somebody would fall in, despite the fences and steep concrete banks and would spark a dramatic rescue effort which, more often than not, failed. It made great TV nonetheless.

The flood basin beneath the spillway, so rarely filled with water, was now overflowing with people. It was one thousand acres of open space and that was the only place anyone felt safe now.

As Marty came down from the Sepulveda Pass, he could see the dam, and the flood of people, just beyond where the San Diego Freeway merged with the Ventura Freeway. He wanted to avoid the tangle of unstable overpasses that converged there and so he climbed off the freeway as it came down the base of the north slope of the Santa Monica Mountains.

He trudged down the embankment onramp alongside the freeway, then followed the street below to the stately, ranch-style homes along Woodvale and Haskell, with their collapsed chimneys, crumbling stucco, and fractured wood siding.

This was where most of the valley money was, in the gentle foothills above Ventura Boulevard and up the hillside to Mulholland. While Hancock Park and Beverly Hills was mostly old money, as old as money could be in Los Angeles, the valley was where the newly-minted TV, movie, sports, and software millionaires built their modest estates, at least by old money standards.

The old money felt when the valley rich had real money, and actually mattered, they'd move to one of the Bs—Brentwood, Beverly Hills, or Bel-Air. Until then, they deserved the valley.

Marty reached Ventura Boulevard and, having seen the thoroughfare after the Northridge Quake in '94, felt like he was looking at a rerun. The buildings on either side of the valley's "main street" had lost their faces, revealing their plaster sinew and iron skeletons. The sidewalks were buckled, the roadway rife with fissures. Broken glass, chunks of mortar, and loose papers were everywhere.

Ventura Boulevard, which ran along the entire southern edge of the valley, was one long, charm-less stretch of fast food franchises, gas stations, grocery stores, car washes, and countless, bland strip malls, with their interchangeable mix of hair salons and donut shops, dry cleaners and locksmiths, liquor stores, copy centers, and video rental places. Culturally and architecturally, no one would miss what had been destroyed, yet again.

The devastation here seemed different to Marty somehow from what he saw on the other side of the hill. It was if he was seeing it all in more detail, under more intense light. He thought perhaps the flatness of the valley and the paucity of tall buildings had something to do with it, allowing the light to spread into corners and cracks it couldn't Downtown or in Hollywood.

Or maybe it was because, unlike the LA basin, he considered this home. Maybe he saw more because he knew the landscape better. As he moved slowly westward, he was aware of so many details that he'd missed before: The sour smell of rotting food. The broken parking meters lying on the street, leaving a spray of glittering change. The concrete bus benches flung into the center of the street by the force of the quake and broken in two. The layer of dust coating everything like powdered sugar. The steady stream of liquor, milk, juice, and soda flowing from shattered mini-marts. The flies swarming over the dead. The overturned mailboxes and the hundreds of letters blowing in the breeze like leaves. And, most of all, the silence.

Everything that had been wailing in the hours immediately following the quake, the car alarms and the injured people, had long since died. All he heard now was the buzz of flies, the rhythmic chopping of a helicopter in the distance and the gentle flap of banners advertising the "Circus Valdez" that fluttered from tilted street lights up and down the boulevard.

Something made him stop suddenly, just west of the intersection of Reseda and Ventura, and he didn't know what it was.

He looked around. A woman stapled a hand-written "Lost Dog-Reward" flier to a listing palm tree.

No, that wasn't it.

About fifty people, some of them barely able to stand because of their injuries, were lined up outside a Tobacco-For-Less store, where cigarettes were being sold out of cardboard crates.

The pathetic sight was worth a glance, but not a full stop.

What the hell was it that grabbed him, instinctively or subliminally, and forced him to halt?

Marty scanned the street. A guy sat on the curb outside a travel

Lee Goldberg

agency, flipping through a Hawaii brochure. Someone had nailed a piece of plywood over their falafel place and spray-painted the words: "Welcome to Tarzana, Some Assembly Required." A couple kids were carting a big screen TV out of a crumbled storefront.

His eyes went back to the plywood sign.

Yeah, it was kind of clever, but it was more clever when he saw the same joke after the '94 quake. That couldn't be what caught his attention. What else was there?

People had dragged some couches out of a furniture store and were sleeping on them in the street. A realtor in his bright orange jacket was sweeping up the broken glass outside of his office, as if he was actually expecting some business. A woman was picking through the rubble at a dry cleaners, carefully sorting the clothes, no doubt looking for her own. A guy was getting his wife and kids to pose in the street for a picture, something to remember the earthquake by in case they forgot.

His gaze returned to the plywood sign. Again.

What was it with the sign? "Welcome to Tarzana, Some Assembly Required."

Yes, he was in Tarzana, formerly author Edgar Rice Burrough's country estate, long since sub-divided and divided again. A city named after a fictional, tree-swinging, raised-by-apes hero. Tacky, but so what? It was just a place he drove through on the way home, an exit off the freeway, he didn't know anybody here.

Yes, you do.

Then he remembered and he knew why he stopped.

Marty reached into his pocket and pulled out the photograph Molly tried to give him. The photo of her five-year-old daughter, Clara. And he remembered what she said, as she was bleeding to death in her car.

"She's at Dandelion Preschool in Tarzana, you'll call the school from the hospital, let them know what happened?"

And she showed him the photo. The same one she tried to give him when the shaking started again. The photo he wouldn't take because he was running away, leaving Molly to die. She screamed for him.

"Angel!"

He was almost home. Dandelion Preschool was out of his way. Clara wasn't his responsibility.

Marty looked down Ventura Boulevard. He was so close to

Beth now. Five, maybe six miles, then his ordeal would be over and they would be together again. That was the whole point of the journey, wasn't it? To get back to his wife, to fight for her, and their marriage, again?

No, it was to get home. It wasn't about their marriage, about fighting for anything, at least not when he started.

But he knew it was now. Somewhere along the way, the destination of his journey had changed.

Now that he thought about it, Marty could almost pinpoint the moment. It was when he met Buck. Almost from the start, Buck challenged him about who he was, how truthful he was with himself and with his wife, forced him to all but admit that he was a lousy husband and that his marriage was falling apart.

And now Marty knew why. He supposed he always knew, he just never admitted it to himself. Their marriage was dying because he gave up his dream of writing and hers of being a mother. He knew the reason he stopped trying to have a kid was the same reason he stopped writing. The obstacles were too much. He couldn't deal with the failure.

But in the last two days, he'd overcome obstacles he would have found impossible to face before. Now the blank page and the empty semen cup didn't seem nearly so frightening any more.

He wasn't the same Martin Slack that he was before, he knew that now. And if he was going to prove it to Beth, he had to prove it to himself first.

5 :11 p.m. Wednesday
The page Marty tore out of the phone book said that Dandelion Preschool was on Kittridge, which meant that technically it wasn't in Tarzana at all, not that it made any difference now.

He didn't have a map anymore, but he headed north on Wilbur because he vaguely remembered seeing a Kittridge street sign before, on his way to Costco, the warehouse store where Beth liked to buy things in bulk, not because they needed that much of anything, but because she couldn't resist. It was like asking her take one potato chip from the bowl when she could have a handful instead. They were still using the same five-pound container of seasoned salt they bought there two years ago, and they probably still would be for years to come.

They didn't take Wilbur to Costco, they took Tampa several blocks west, but this was the first north-south street he came across and he knew that if Kittridge crossed Tampa, and you could say the school was in Tarzana, then it had to cross Wilbur, too.

Marty didn't know what he was going to say or do when he got to the school, but he knew he had to go there. Molly's dying wish, even if it was implied rather than said, was that he save her girl. If Clara was even alive. And what if she wasn't at the school anymore? What would he do then? How long and how far would he search before going home?

He didn't have a chance to answer those questions right away, because he was immediately distracted by two things. First, was the Los Angeles River, which he could see to his left and right, which meant that he was over it and that the street he was on was actually a bridge. He'd been so lost in his thoughts, he hadn't even realized he was walking on a bridge. But he considered his alternative. The banks of the river were nearly vertical slabs of concrete. If he didn't take one of the streets over it, he'd have had to back-track all the way to Balboa Park near the Sepulveda Dam, scale the dry river bed, then come back this direction. He probably would have chosen this route anyway.

That's what he thought, and tried to tell himself, in the split second between his first distraction, and the second one, which made the first all the more horrifying:

The aftershock.

The center of the overpass collapsed, turning both ends into immense, concrete slides. Marty rolled and tumbled, along with a dozen other people, two cars, and one motorcycle, down towards the concrete river bed below.

CHAPTER FOURTEEN
How Green Was My Valley

T he valley?" Marty couldn't understand what Beth was thinking. She might as well have suggested they move to Fresno. "Why would you want to move there?"

"Because you can get twice the house for the money," Beth replied.

"That's because no one wants to live there."

"Michael Jackson lives in Encino."

"I rest my case."

They were renting a house in Westwood, two blocks south of Wilshire Boulevard, for $2200-a-month. The neighborhood didn't have the cachet it once did, but when Marty walked the dog he still bumped into character actors, up-and-coming directors, and C-list screenwriters, and that was nice.

"Marty, for what it costs to buy an old, two-bedroom fixer-upper in Santa Monica we can go to the valley and get a new, four-bedroom Mediterranean mansion with a swimming pool and a huge yard in a gated community," she said. "And, best of all, we won't have to send our children to private school."

"We don't have any children."

"We will," she said. "That should be the criteria for choosing where we live, not whether it's a hip place."

"The valley has no character. It's just shopping centers and freeways and tract homes. It will be like living in one of those rest stops on the interstate," Marty argued. "What's wrong with the Hollywood Hills or one of the canyons, off Coldwater, for instance? Or how about the Palisades, Hancock Park, or Brentwood?"

"Forget about the hills and canyons. I don't want to be living on the edge of a cliff when the next quake comes. Besides, those houses have no yards at all and are on narrow, steep streets. Hancock Park, the Palisades, and Brentwood cost too much for too little, and we'd still have to send our kids to private school at $12,000-a-year-per-child," Beth said. "I also want to know our children can play in the front yard and be safe, and in a gated community, you've got some measure of security."

"So, in other words, you want to live in a country club prison out in the boonies," Marty replied. "If we're going to do time, let's at least try to embezzle some money or rob a bank first, so we've actually earned the punishment."

"I want the most for our money and the safest possible neighborhood for our family," Beth said firmly. "You want a place you can brag about over lunch at Le Guerre, so when agents messenger you scripts at home for a weekend read they'll be impressed by the zip code. Jesus, Marty, where are your priorities?"

He looked at Beth's face. Her eyes were blazing with anger and stubborn determination. She was already a mother-bear protecting her cubs, and she didn't even have any yet.

How could Marty argue against getting more for their money, the best schools for their kids, and security for his family? He couldn't. She knew it and so did he. It was an infuriating position for him to be in.

Who cares that the valley was numbingly dull, choked with smog, and one evolutionary step above a vast trailer park? No matter what he said in opposition, he'd come off like an asshole.

Beth was always doing this to him, framing an argument in just the right way so he got trapped every time. Either that, or he was a genuine asshole, and he didn't like that possibility.

Okay, so he did care what people thought about his zip code. What's so bad about that? After all, part of being a husband and father was being a good provider, and the wrong address, the wrong car, the wrong clothes, or the wrong table at a restaurant could have a severe impact on his industry credibility and, eventually, his advancement prospects and salary. And, by extension, the lifestyle he could provide his loved ones.

Image was the only thing that mattered in his business and yes, damn it, what other people thought about where he lived was important. But he couldn't admit that now, not when she had fiscal and parental responsibility on her side.

So he gave up.

It was just a house, and he was at the network most of the time anyway, which was why they could afford to buy a place. He'd just have to stay late on Fridays, that's all, and refuse to allow anything to be messengered to his home. He'd say his home was sacrosanct. The idea suddenly appealed to him. A rule like that would make him look even more powerful.

Yeah, he thought, I'm an asshole and pretty successful at it, too.

Marty sighed heavily and smiled in that lovable way he knew she liked. "Does this mean I have to trade my Lexus in for a Volvo wagon?"

She smiled back. "Not yet."

He put his arms around her and pulled her close. "Have you ever seen *Chinatown*?"

"All I remember is that Jack Nicholson gets his nose cut and slaps Faye Dunaway around until she admits she's his mother and his sister or something like that."

"Then we better go rent it," he turned her around and led her to the front door. "If we're going to live in the valley, you'd better know its secrets."

5:13 p.m. Wednesday
There was water in the Los Angeles River after all, and it was warm.

That was the first sensation Marty became aware of, the next was the intense pain radiating from his right side. Every breath brought a new stab of agony. He guessed broken ribs, because he'd suffered that before, falling off a dirt bike when he was eighteen, and it didn't hurt this bad. That was two only two broken ribs, maybe all his ribs were broken this time. He was barely aware of his scorched back. He'd traded up to this new torture, which was so strong, it demanded all his attention, blotting out the discomfort of his other injuries.

The instinctive part of his brain was doing a quick systems check, his synapses firing back responses from all over his body, reports filtering up through his consciousness. He tried to wiggle his toes and flex his fingers and was relieved that he could and without feeling any new pain. At least he wasn't paralyzed. A visual inspection was required now and he was afraid of what he would see.

Marty opened his eyes and saw blue sky and half of the Wilbur overpass sloping down towards him, tiny pebbles of asphalt rolling down its cracked surface and spilling onto him.

He slowly lifted his head so he could see his body, knowing it was probably a mistake, that he'd widen the hairline fracture in his neck and paralyze himself for life, but he couldn't resist. Marty had to know what was causing his pain.

His neck didn't break, but what he saw made him gasp in shock. There were three inches of bloody rebar poking through his side. The warm wetness he was feeling wasn't water, it was blood. He was stuck on a piece of exposed iron from the snapped support pillar.

If that was true, then why wasn't he feeling the hard, jagged surface of the mortar under his back? Whatever he was lying on was soft and squishy.

Marty looked over his right shoulder. The blood he was soaked with was only partly his own. He was on the end of a human shish-ka-bob, the rebar impaling Marty and the several people beneath him who had cushioned his fall. He was sorry they were dead, but at the same time, knew if they hadn't died, every bone in his body would be broken. The thing to do was not to think about them or that it was their guts sticking to his back.

He looked to his left, and saw a crumpled Buick Regal only inches from him and realized things could be much, much worse. He could've been under that.

"Help!" he yelled, and immediately felt a blinding, teeth-grinding wave of pain that almost made him faint.

No one's going to come for you. There are families trapped under houses. Neighborhoods in flame. Who gives a shit about some guy stuck on a spike in the LA river?

He looked to either side again, and then he listened. The only moans he heard were his own. He was alone. His walk was over and probably his life, too.

Marty closed his eyes. It was almost laughable. He'd survived so much, only to be taken out just a few, short miles from home. All because he'd strayed from his path to find a little girl he didn't even know.

And Beth would never know why he died. She'd always wonder how he ended up speared in that river bed, so close to home, with a snapshot of two strangers in his pocket. If only he had a pen, he could write it all down, tell Beth so the story would be resolved. But this story would remain unfinished, just like every other one he ever tried to tell. There was a certain ironic justice to that.

A rock pinged into the car, right above his head, startling him into opening his eyes. Was this more loose rubble, or was the rest of the bridge about to fall on him now? He stared at the cracked asphalt, willing it not to move.

Another rock hit the car, near his head again, but he was certain it didn't come from above, because he was watching. This rock came from an angle. Someone threw it.

"Hey Marty," a voice yelled, "wake the fuck up."

He turned his head, looked up to his right and saw a figure standing on the edge of the high, vertical riverbank.

It couldn't be.

Marty blinked hard and squinted at the trick of the light.

"I knew you were alive," Buck yelled happily. "You're the luckiest damn guy I've ever met. Now, are you going to lie there all day feeling sorry for yourself or are you going to get up?"

It was one of those utterly improbable and convenient coincidences that he railed against every time he came across them in a script, an undeniable hallmark of weak plotting and hack writing. And yet there Buck Weaver was, like a western hero, the sun behind his back, casting his long shadow across the concrete river.

Marty smiled. "Buck, what are you doing here?"

"Saving your skinny ass."

"What are you waiting for?" Marty replied, "Get down here and do it."

"That's not exactly the plan I had in mind."

"Then what's your plan?"

158

"My plan is that you get up off your ass, like I said."

For a moment, Marty's anger actually eclipsed his crippling pain. "I'm impaled on a fucking piece of rebar. Why don't you come down here and help me?"

"Because I'm not fucking Spiderman. These banks are totally vertical, so that's out, and if I try climbing down that bridge, I could bring it all down on top of you, not to mention. I suppose I could go all the way back to Balboa Park and walk up the canal from there, but you'll probably bleed to death before I get back. So you might as well get off your ass. You're fucked no matter what."

Marty closed his eyes and groaned. He felt the blood pulsing out of his wound. "And then what am I supposed to do?"

"Walk to the park and climb out of the river."

Marty had to laugh, even though the slightest motion of his stomach caused a new wave of pain. "I got a better idea. You go find help. I'll wait here."

"There isn't any help. I'm it. And I'm telling you to get up. Be a fucking man."

Be a fucking man.

Of course, Marty thought, why didn't I think of that. "How did you find me?"

"We can have a fucking chat when you're on your feet," Buck yelled angrily. "Now get up, goddamn it! You can't catch fish with your line in the boat."

"What did you say?"

"You heard me. Get up!"

Marty didn't know how to lift himself off the spike, and even if he did, he was afraid the pain would be so bad, he'd fall right back on it again, impaling himself somewhere else even worse. He was also afraid of how much it would hurt, though it was hard to imagine anything hurting more than it already did.

"How am I supposed to do this, Buck?"

"Grab the car with one hand, use the other to steady yourself. Then bend your knees, plant your feet, and use your hands and legs to simultaneously lift and push yourself up. Nothing to it."

It sounded like the most complicated physical procedure Marty had ever heard. At this moment, Olympic gymnastics seemed simpler to perform. But Buck was right, Marty had no choice, unless he wanted to stay there and bleed to death.

With his left hand, Marty grabbed hold of the car, made sure he had a firm grip, then placed his right hand flat beside him and tried not to think about what the spongy surface was under his palm. Then he drew his knees up, which caused him to slightly shift position. The bolt of pain that shot from his wound took his breath away.

"I don't think I can do this," Marty whispered to himself. Somehow, though, Buck heard him.

"I read about this Texas Ranger in the old west, got himself captured by the Mexicans. You know what they did to him? They made him stick an arm into this knothole that went through a pecan tree. They put a big rock in his hand, then tied his fist shut around it so he couldn't pull his arm back through the knothole. They left him like that for the wolves or the Indians or whatever. You know what that tough bastard did? Cut his own arm off with a pocket knife and dragged himself 40 miles to the nearest settlement. And you're complaining about one, lousy sliver in your flab?"

Put like that, his problems did seem a bit petty. Marty counted to three and did it.

The agony was excruciating. He screamed, the rebar sliding out of him with a moist squish. It felt like half his guts came out with it, too. Just before he fainted against the Buick, he imagined his intestines trailing out behind him, tangled in the pipe.

For a moment, he was just floating, the pain was gone, and he was blissfully calm. Then his consciousness came back, pushed forward by a stampede of pain that pounded through his body.

His eyes flashed open again.

"See, that wasn't so bad," Buck said.

"My side is killing me."

"You got to walk it off, like a cramp."

Marty tried to stand up straight, but the pain was so bad, he started to see lights in his eyes, like flashbulbs going off. He blinked hard, his vision cleared, and he stumbled around the bloody spike, trying not to look at the other bodies impaled on it. He staggered into the river bed, clutching his side, feeling the blood coursing between his fingers.

"I'm gonna bleed to death, Buck."

"Probably," Buck replied from the bank. "Shove your shirt into the wound and press as hard as you can, try to stop the bleeding."

"It's going to hurt."

"It already hurts, how much worse can it get?"

"Easy for you to say."

Marty untucked his shirt, gathered up his shirt-tails, and crammed the fabric against his wound. It was like sticking another spike in his flesh. He whimpered.

"Press harder, Marty."

"It hurts," Marty yelled, nearly crying.

"It's better than being dead, goddamn it. Now hold it tight against the wound and start walking."

Marty hugged the concrete bank to his right, staggered under the tunnel created by the fallen section of overpass, and then he just kept going, dragging his shoulder along the wall, using it as a support to prop himself up.

Above him, Buck followed along. "When we get to the park, you can follow some of the medical advice I gave you at the field hospital."

"You want me to look for horsehair to put in the wound?"

"Horseshit would be better, but mud will do."

This talk about the field hospital and treating his wound raised an obvious question. What was Buck doing here?

"So now will you tell me how you found me?"

"I wasn't looking for you. I was looking for Clara Hobart."

Marty looked up at Buck, but from his angle against the concrete wall, he couldn't see Buck's face, just the shadow he cast as he followed him. "How did you know about Clara?"

"You told me."

"I did?"

"It was one of your rants explaining why you didn't have to do a fucking thing for anybody because you already did your heroic deed for that kid's mother," Buck replied. "But since Molly's toast, and you technically did nothing heroic, I said it didn't count. Saving her kid would count."

"I don't remember having that conversation."

"You wouldn't, selfish bastard, which is why I decided to come here and do it for you. I figured you'd forget about her. So, as you can imagine, I nearly shit myself when I saw you down there."

"I know I didn't say anything to you about Dandelion Preschool."

"You didn't have to, I'm a licensed investigator and bounty

hunter. This is what I do for a living. I saw the kid was wearing a Dandelion Preschool t-shirt in the picture you're carrying around, so I deduced, as the crack investigative professional that I am, that she might be enrolled there."

"I never showed you the picture."

"I saw it when I was going through your pockets."

Marty was outraged. "You went through my pockets? When?"

"While you were sleeping in the office building. It was the first chance I had and I was curious."

"About what?"

"How the fuck do I know? I go through everyone's pockets. It's what I do."

Marty wanted to throttle the infuriating, son-of-a-bitch. And then he had a startling realization, in his anger, he'd all but forgotten his pain. Buck had managed to distract him from it, which made Marty wonder if that wasn't Buck's intention to start with. Then again, maybe he was crediting Buck with more cleverness than the Neanderthal could possibly possess. And now that Marty had made himself conscious of the distraction, the pain came rushing back full force. He went against his better judgment and decided to encourage Buck to piss him off some more.

"What happened to staying and helping Angie?" Marty asked.

"She's a lesbo," Buck said, as if that explained everything. In a way, it did, but for medicinal purposes Marty wasn't going to let it go.

"How do you know she's a lesbian?"

"It's obvious."

"If it's obvious," Marty asked, "why did you bother hitting on her?"

"Because if there was any hetero left in her, and there was, I could have brought it out."

"You thought one look at you would unleash the lusty heterosexual trapped inside her."

"Sometimes it takes longer. Instinctively, she wanted me. She couldn't hide it. But making her realize it would have taken too much time. I've been through it before. It's hard work, but in the end it's worth it. There's nothing hornier than a freed lesbo. Bottom line is, no matter what they say, they all want dick."

"Specifically, your dick."

Buck leaned over the edge of the embankment and gave him a

cold look. "You're mocking me."

Marty looked up at him and smiled. "Yep."

"Do you know why you're mocking me?"

"Because it's fun and it distracts me from my pain?"

"Jealousy, inadequacy, and rage."

"Excuse me?"

"You wish you were as masculine as me and as capable as me and you're pissed at yourself because you know you can't be."

Buck was obviously trying to deflect the conversation away from his defeat, but Marty was determined not to let that happen.

"You're partly right," Marty replied. "I know I will never have your ego or arrogance. But here's where you're wrong: I don't want it. I don't want to intimidate or offend everyone I meet. I'd like to have some friends."

"Like that producer guy we met?"

"That was an unusual situation," replied Marty defensively, knowing his argument was slipping away from him and, with it, the fun he was hoping to have. Suddenly Buck wasn't on the spot any more; he was. That had to be reversed, fast.

"The point I'm making," Marty said, "is all you think about is overpowering people, whether verbally, physically, or with a gun. You get off on intimidation."

"And you don't? You were afraid if that cook saw you in your filthy clothes, some day he'd stick you at a bad table and you'd wouldn't be able to intimidate people into listening to your stupid fucking notes anymore. The difference between you and me is people listen to me because I make 'em, not because some burger flipper tells them to. That's what you envy. You're second-in-command of your own fucking life."

"Allowing other people to have some impact on your life is what gives you a life." Marty said. "That's why you spend your nights alone in bars, collecting napkins to decorate your bathroom with, while I go home to a woman who loves me."

Buck snorted derisively.

"Is that what you think the difference is between us? A woman? Anybody can get a woman. That doesn't mean shit. Being able to be alone, and comfortable with yourself, is a hell of a lot harder. Can you look me in the fucking eye and tell me you're happy with who you are?"

Marty wasn't falling for that one. "Nobody can."

"I can."

"Then you're fooling yourself. You honestly think there's nothing missing from your life?"

"There sure as shit is," Buck said. "A couple thousand cocktail napkins, numerous appliances, a big screen TV, a pristine Mercury Montego, a dozen firearms, and the best fucking dog there ever was."

"Don't you ever get tired of it?"

"Tired of what?"

"Your tough-guy posturing. You know, that guys look at you and tremble in fear or envy. That every woman wants to fuck you, including nuns, grandmothers, lesbians, and the clinically dead. That you're so tough you eat live scorpions for breakfast and wash your mouth out with battery acid. That shit. Did I forget anything?"

"Did it ever occur to you that I'm telling it to you exactly the way it is? There's no fucking mystery who I am. What I put out there is it. You're the guy who's full of shit, but I think we've already established that more than once."

"Yeah, I guess we have."

That was the last time Marty was going to try and bait Buck, at least until he could figure out a safe way to do it. So far, the conversation always ended up turning around and biting Marty in the ass instead, and that was certainly no fun. Buck was like Beth in that way. It was like they took the same "How to Neuter Marty Slack" course.

They walked for a few minutes in silence, except for Marty's occasional moans and groans. Then Buck cleared his throat and spoke.

"Your feet still hurt?"

Marty was holding his guts in with his hand, and Buck was worried about his blisters? But he knew what the remark was really about. It was about apologizing for trashing a guy while he was down and letting Marty know that Buck cared about him.

"Not as much," Marty replied.

"I guess the new shoes helped."

Marty glanced at his sturdy new shoes, now splattered with blood. "I think so."

Buck nodded. "A man needs a solid pair of shoes."

CHAPTER FIFTEEN
Valley Girl

6:26 p.m. Wednesday
As Martin Slack sat on the weedy river bank in Balboa Park, packing a mixture of mud and leaves into his wound, he saw he wasn't hurt quite as bad as he'd imagined.

Marty was afraid he'd have to stuff his oozing intestines back into some gaping, gory hole in his stomach. Instead, it looked like the rebar left a clean puncture about a half-inch around, swollen and red, straight through one of his "love handles." He didn't have to shove a perforated kidney or some other internal organs back into place after all. Then again, for all he knew, birds were fighting over meaty chunks of his appendix in the river bed right now.

The cool dirt made his wound feel better, and staunched the bleeding, but he couldn't help wondering if it was promoting an infection at the same time. It was dirt. Weren't you supposed to keep that out of open wounds? Then again, infection was hardly his immediate concern. All he really wanted to do now was stop the bleeding and diminish his pain so he could get home. So far, there were noticeable improvements on both fronts.

Buck studied the poultice and nodded with approval. "That's

gonna make for one manly scar."

"Something to go with the bullet wound," Marty said.

"Now that you've got some hard-living on your doughy flesh, you won't look like such a wimp anymore. You may have to consider a new line of work."

"I already am."

Buck grinned. "I don't usually take on apprentices, but I can make an exception in your case."

"That's a nice offer, Buck. But I was thinking of something more sedentary."

"You want to be a gardener?"

"I said sedentary not sedimentary," Marty replied. "I'm going to be a writer."

"A writer would choose his words more carefully to avoid confusion," Buck said. "Maybe you ought to look into a field that already matches your skills. You know, like car salesman or telemarketer."

Marty ignored the remark. He picked up a sturdy tree limb he'd found on the bank and, using it for support, lifted himself up into a standing position, gasping with pain. It felt like his back and his side were competing with each other to be the most agonizing.

Now that Marty was standing, he could see the mass of earthquake refugees that surrounded the man-made lake in the center of the park on the other side of the river. It looked like they'd gathered for an outdoor rock concert. And, in the distance beyond them, he could see thousands more people filling the public golf course, which every few years would flood so suddenly and so completely, stranded golfers had to be plucked out of the trees by helicopters.

"I sure could use something to drink," Marty said. "My throat feels as dry as that river."

Buck motioned to a Red Cross tent in middle of the flood of people. "They've probably got water."

Marty considered the distance, and the complications that would arise if the Red Cross workers saw his wound, and shook his head no. "I'd rather use the energy to get closer to home. Besides, we still have one more stop to make. C'mon, let's go."

"You sure you can make it?" Buck looked at him skeptically. "Maybe you'd be better off quitting and flopping on a cot in that Red Cross tent."

"I've been quitting and flopping for too long already." Marty hobbled off grimacing towards Victory Boulevard, leaning heavily on his walking stick.

Buck looked after him thoughtfully for a moment, then fell into step beside him.

6:50 p.m. Wednesday
After World War II, service men flush with GI loans all wanted their square footage of the American dream and came looking for it in the San Fernando Valley. Developers manufactured the dream with assembly-line precision, economy, and sameness, coating the valley with ranch-style homes that offered easy-living in harmony with nature, what little of it hadn't been graded and paved over.

Every home Marty and Buck passed looked the same, with their plywood siding and low-pitched, wood-shake roofs, bird houses built into the over-hanging eaves or perched on top like little cupolas to add that extra touch of prefabricated charm. On many houses, the roofs stretched to detached garages or carports, creating breezeways which, in later years, were widely converted into cheap additions by amateur carpenters.

Dandelion Preschool still looked like the rambling, free-flowing ranch house it once was, only with several room additions and a high cyclone fence surrounding a broad front yard long since turned into a parking lot.

The school's plywood sign, decorated with bad renderings of famous cartoon characters, dangled from the collapsed front porch, and a crack ran around the house where it met the raised foundation. But beyond that, and other superficial cracking, the house appeared to have come through the quake fairly well, raising Marty's hopes that Clara might be alive and unhurt.

Marty stood out front, gathering his courage, trying to think of what he was going to say to Clara and the teachers inside. But he was so tired, and hurt so much, he was finding it difficult to concentrate. The only thing he could think of doing was asking for some water and a place to lie down.

"Maybe I ought to handle this," Buck said, studying Marty's haggard face.

"This is my problem."

"Yeah, but I have a better chance of walking out of there with the kid."

"Why do you say that?"

"Look at you, Marty. You're a fuckin' nightmare and you smell like a bucket of shit. You're gonna frighten the teacher and the kid," Buck explained. "Besides, if the teacher doesn't cooperate, I'll just snatch the kid. I'm big and I'm armed. You couldn't stand up to a puff of air."

Marty knew that logically Buck was right but it didn't make any difference to him. "I have to do this, Buck. Alone. If I don't come out with Clara, we can have another discussion."

"Fuck that, you don't come out with the kid I'll go in and get her."

Marty decided to conserve his energy and fight that battle with Buck when, and if, it was necessary. So he just nodded, opened the gate, and walked around the side of the house to the back yard.

The narrow pathway led to a weather-beaten, wood fence and was clogged with discarded playground toys: building blocks, balls of all sizes, tricycles, pedal cars, plastic buckets, and shovels. Working his way through the mess and trying not to stumble was killing him. Each twist around an object or big step over one felt like he was getting speared again.

He stopped to ride out a wave of pain and heard the laughter and squeals of children playing, which both surprised and enchanted him. It was odd, and yet magical, to hear such gaiety amidst such a disaster. He moved toward the sounds, drawn almost hypnotically, and in his haste, slipped on a tiny toy fire engine.

Marty yelped in pain and fell against a plastic slide, which sent a tricycle careening into the fence with a noisy clatter.

A woman rushed over from the back of the house, threw open the gate, and just stood there, clearly unsure what she should do next. She was about forty, wore shorts and a wrinkled Dandelion Preschool t-shirt, and regarded him with cried-out brown eyes that were underscored with deep, dark circles of worry and fatigue. Marty saw the questions passing across her weary face. Do I run away? Do I help him? Or do I find a weapon to defend myself and the children?

It wasn't easy for her to make a judgment. She'd reached her limit of unexpected situations and difficult choices and was emotionally tapped out. Marty could sympathize.

168

"I'll make it easy for you," Marty groaned as he struggled to his feet. "There's no reason to be afraid of me. The only reason I'm here is to pick up one of the kids, Clara Hobart."

She eyed him suspiciously. "Are you her father?"

"No. I'm a family friend."

"Is something wrong, Faye?" a man's voice called out from behind her.

"I haven't decided yet," Faye replied.

"Why don't you decide back here where I can see you and whoever you're talking to," the man said.

She stepped aside and then, as an afterthought, held open the gate so Marty could hobble past her.

The large backyard had been turned into a playground. Three kids ran around a swing set and jungle-gym. The two boys and Clara froze when they saw the stranger come in and swallowed their laughter, their little stomachs going in and out as they tried to catch their breath.

Clara looked like her photo, but there was a difference he wasn't prepared for. It wasn't the matching scrapes on her knees, or her braided pony-tail, or even her radiant blue eyes. She had a band of freckles over her nose.

Just like Beth. No, exactly like Beth's.

He didn't see that in the photo, or he would have fallen in love with Clara long before that instant.

There was no way he was going to leave without her.

The man who'd called out to Faye sat on a bench, his left leg in a crude splint made out of duct tape and two fence slats. He saw Marty looking at his leg.

"A bookcase fell on me, broke my leg like a twig."

"I think the whole world fell on me," Marty replied, noticing a jug of water and some paper cups on the picnic table.

"Looks like it, too if you don't mind me saying so," The man said with a friendly smile and a soft voice that reminded Marty of Mister Rogers. "I'm Alan Plebney, the headmaster of Dandelion Preschool; this is my wife Faye."

"I'm Martin Slack," he said, returning the smile. Things were getting off to a good start. "May I have some water?"

"Help yourself."

Marty guzzled down four cups and half expected to see it all leaking out of the hole in his gut. Instead, the water flowed through him like an electric charge.

"Where are the other teachers?" Marty asked.

"I let them go home to their families. As headmaster, I have to stay until all the children are returned to their parents. Besides, I can't go anywhere with this leg anyway." He motioned to his wife and his eyes glowed with admiration. "My wife walked all the way here from Studio City to make sure me and the children were okay."

Marty glanced at Faye, and saw her having a muffled conversation with Clara. The little girl looked fearfully back at him, a look that wasn't lost on either Faye or her husband.

"How do you know Clara?" Alan asked protectively.

Marty decided to go with honesty. "I don't."

"Then I'm afraid I don't understand what you're doing here, Mr. Slack, besides having a couple cups of water."

Marty reached into his pocket, took out the singed picture of Molly and Clara, and whispered as he showed it to Alan. "Her mother gave this to me. Just before she died."

Alan glanced over at Clara, then back to him.

"She asked me to take care of her daughter," Marty said. "That's why I'm here."

"Were you a close friend?" Alan asked.

"Not until that moment."

Alan took a deep breath and let it out slowly. "I can't let this child go with a complete stranger, no matter how well intentioned he may be."

"Is there any one else? Did Molly give you a name of someone she trusted as an emergency contact?" Marty asked, but he already knew the answer.

Alan shook his head. "She said she had to think about it. That was three months ago."

Faye rejoined them, leaving Clara with her friends.

"You can't let this man take her, Alan," she said firmly, then lowered her voice so Clara couldn't hear. "He could be a child molester."

"Take a good look at me, Mrs. Plebney," Marty said. "Do I look like I'm in any shape to hurt anyone?"

From the expressions on their faces, he knew he'd scored a point with that. Marty reached into his pocket, took out his wallet, and handed them his driver's license. "This is me. You keep it. If anyone else comes for Clara, you can tell them that's who has her and that's where she is. But we both know that's not going to happen."

Alan took his license and studied it, as if the answer to this problem was written on it in very fine print.

"I walked here from downtown Los Angeles, carrying that picture in my pocket. Along the way, I've been shot, poisoned, burned, impaled, and nearly drowned. I want to go home to my wife now, and I'd like to bring Clara with me. I don't know if my house is still there, or if my wife is even alive. But I promise you, no matter what I find, Clara will be safe. I will take care of her."

Alan and Faye Plebney stared at him, wrestling with the decision. And while they were, Clara came up and touched the picture in Alan's hand.

"That's my mommy," Clara said. "Is she coming to get me soon?"

"She asked me to get you, Clara," Marty spoke up quickly, before the Plebneys could answer. "My name is Martin."

Clara looked up hesitantly at Marty. She wanted to believe him. "What's the secret word?"

"Please," he replied.

"No, the other secret word," Clara said.

Marty had no idea what it was.

The Plebneys and Clara were staring at him, waiting. Like it was a challenge. Like they all knew he didn't know.

Why didn't Molly tell him? She had to know her kid would ask.

"She said not to go with a stranger who doesn't know the secret word," Clara repeated, just in case he needed reminding.

In a few seconds, Clara was going to turn against him, and then the Plebneys would follow suit. Marty couldn't let that stop him, even if it meant calling in Buck and using force. Because if Marty didn't leave with Clara, he'd be haunted for the rest of his life with that last image of Molly, holding that picture out to him, her eyes pleading, calling to him with her last breath . . .

And by remembering that, what didn't make sense before now was perfectly clear. Molly did tell him.

"Angel," Marty said.

Clara nodded.

"Is that the secret word?" Alan asked Clara gently.

"Yes," she said, then looked up at Marty with big, wishful eyes.

"Will you take me to see my Mommy?"

Marty looked at the Plebneys. It was up to them now.

Alan glanced at his wife, who gave her nod of acceptance, then he turned to Clara. "Martin is going to take care of you for a while."

"Where's my Mommy?" Clara asked, stuffing the burnt, wrinkled picture into her pocket.

The three adults shared an awkward moment of silence. None of them wanted to tell Clara the horrible news yet. Some day soon, perhaps even today, Marty would have to tell Clara that her mother was dead. And on another day, a long time from now, he would have to tell her how her mother died and all the things she said to him. Eventually, he'd have to hurt her and it was a pain he knew would never go away, for either of them.

"We don't know," Alan replied. "But we know that wherever she is, she loves you and wants you to be safe. That's why she sent Martin to take you home."

Faye gave Clara a kiss on the top of her head. "That's from me and Mr. Plebney. You've been a very, very good girl. Now you have to be a good girl with Martin too. We'll see you soon."

Clara nodded shyly.

Marty held his hand out to Clara. "We're going on a long walk, but I've got a problem. I hurt myself and I need someone to help me. Would you be my helper?"

She nodded and took his hand.

He squeezed her hand and let her lead him out again through the sideyard.

They found Buck pacing nervously out front, waiting for them. Buck flashed Clara his biggest, most winning smile.

"This is my friend Buck," Marty said. "He's going to walk with us."

"So this is the beautiful princess I've heard so much about," Buck said. "You are even more enchanting than I imagined, your highness."

Buck did an elaborate bow. Clara didn't say anything. She was obviously intimidated. Marty couldn't really blame her.

"See those big shoulders? You know what they're for?" Marty asked. "Giving beautiful, little princesses rides so they don't get tired on long walks. Would you like him to give you a ride?"

She shook her head no. "You said you wanted me to help."

172

"So I did," Marty turned to Buck. "Sorry."

Buck flashed his smile at Clara again. "Well, if you change your mind, your Highness, you just snap your fingers."

The three of them walked in silence for an hour, working their way west on Ventura Boulevard as darkness fell. Marty was afraid to say anything to her for fear it would lead back to questions about her mother.

Silence was much safer.

Each step was more painful than the last, but feeling her tiny hand in his somehow made him feel stronger, that he could take on anything if that's what it took to keep her safe. With just that touch, his own life took second place to hers.

Clara unknowingly emboldened him when they came to the inevitable moment when they had to cross the LA river again. He didn't want to show any hesitancy or fear in front of her, so he simply hustled her across the overpass as quickly as he could without fainting from the pain.

If Buck sensed any of this, he kept quiet about it, but not silent. He whistled Disney tunes as they walked. Marty didn't know if it made Clara feel better, but it helped him. He wished Buck had started whistling downtown instead of talking. The whole journey would have been a lot more pleasant.

The moon shone brightly over the frontier storefronts and wood-plank sidewalks of old town Calabasas, a collection of over-priced restaurants, antique stores, and real estate offices. The small street was designed to replicate the ambience of the stagecoach stop that existed there in the 1860s. Despite its genuine historical underpinnings, the street still looked like an abandoned movie set and, as it turned out, was about as sturdy. Against the quake, the buildings folded up flat like cardboard boxes. The wood planks of the sidewalk splintered violently, snapping with such force that torn boards were thrown into the trees, snagging in the branches.

But this wasn't the real Calabasas, which was more appropriately symbolized a few blocks further west by a Mediterranean-style shopping center that boasted the world's largest Rolex timepiece, mounted over a Ralph's Supermarket that had its own full-time sushi chef.

They were so close to home now, Marty wondered if Beth would hear him if he screamed her name.

"We're almost home," Marty said excitedly.

Clara stopped. "You said you were taking me home."

"I am," he said.

"But I don't live here."

Marty looked at her and suddenly realized the terrible misunderstanding they had. They were so close to home, in a few minutes it wouldn't have mattered. Why couldn't he keep his big mouth shut?

"I'm taking you to my house," he said as sweetly as he could.

"I want to go home," Clara said, her little chin trembling, her lips drooping into a frown.

"I know you do. I'm sorry you misunderstood," Marty said to Clara. "Your mommy asked me to take you to my house."

"Why?" she cried.

He looked to Buck, who shrugged helplessly. This was Marty's problem.

"Because she wants you to be safe," Marty replied.

"I want to go home!" Clara jerked her hand away from his and marched off in a crying fury, stomping her feet.

Beth would know how to handle this better than he. She was great with kids. All he had to do was get Clara to go a few more blocks and it would all be over.

Marty turned and whispered to Buck. "Maybe you ought to grab her and carry her the rest of the way."

"I don't know how to carry a child," Buck replied.

"You carry them like a bag of groceries."

"So I hold her by the hair and swing her beside my leg?"

Marty was about to reply when he realized something. He didn't hear Clara crying any more.

He didn't hear her at all.

"Clara?"

Marty turned to see her standing absolutely still a few yards away, staring in horror at the tiger, a dead Labrador in its slavering jaws.

CHAPTER SIXTEEN
The Land of Make-Believe

No.

At first, Marty thought he was hallucinating, then he remembered the circus banners along Ventura Boulevard, and knew this was real. The tiger must have escaped during the quake.

The big animal let out a low, rumbling growl, its eyes locked on Clara.

"Don't move, Clara," Marty whispered, "and don't look into his eyes."

Marty had no idea if that was going to help, but he had to tell her something to make her believe he knew what he has doing.

Buck took out his gun and whispered. "The kid is in the way."

Marty nodded and moved slowly towards her.

The tiger didn't like that, or he decided Clara looked tastier than what he already had. He dropped the dog carcass and growled again, exposing his moist, bloody teeth.

Marty saw that the dog's throat was almost entirely ripped apart, its head barely attached by a few strings of torn flesh. And he couldn't help thinking what those same jaws would do to Clara's neck.

Clara whimpered and stepped back. The tiger advanced slowly, the muscles in his hind legs twitching.

Marty was too far away to reach her. There was only one thing he could do: Make the tiger come for him. It worked in *Jaws 2* for Roy Scheider, who whacked an oar against a 6-million-volt electric line and got the shark to chomp on it. So Marty whacked his stick against the ground and prayed Buck was a good shot.

"Hey, tiger, look at me you ugly son-of-a-bitch."

The tiger did, snarling.

"Yeah, that's it, I'm the one you want," Marty yelled, banging his stick and hobbling towards the animal. "Come and get me if you've got the guts."

The tiger lowered his head and snarled, taking a slow step towards him and away from Clara.

Marty glanced at her and whispered. "Run Clara!"

She did and at the same instant, Marty roared and charged the animal. The tiger pounced. Marty dived to the ground and Buck fired twice, the gunshots sounding like explosions.

The tiger leaped over Marty and kept on running, scrambling into the protection of the bushes and the darkness beyond.

The gunshots were still echoing in Marty's ears as he struggled to his feet, the wound in his side oozing blood again. At least that was the only place he was bleeding. Clara ran to him crying and hugged him as tightly as she could. He wanted to cry too, only with frustration at the malevolent God that was tormenting him.

A tiger? You attacked me with a fucking tiger? Haven't I been through enough already?

Clearly the answer was no. Fate wasn't through with Martin Slack yet. At this point, Marty wouldn't be surprised if he stepped on his front lawn and sank in quicksand.

Buck came up behind them, still holding his gun.

"Thank you, Buck," Marty could feel Clara's little heart pounding.

"That's what the gun is for. Let's get moving. I don't want to be here if Tony the Tiger comes back for his sugar flakes."

Marty straightened up, wincing in pain. His blood had gotten on Clara, but if she noticed, she didn't care. She looked up at him, still trembling, tears rolling down her cheeks.

"I want my mommy."

"I want mine, too." Marty held his hand out to Clara. "You

were very brave, Clara. Can you be brave for me for a little while longer?"

She sniffled and took his hand. Marty gave her a gentle, reassuring squeeze and they started walking, giving the dead dog a wide berth. They also kept a watchful eye out in case the tiger returned or a swarm of locusts happened to show up or a freak tornado touched down. Marty was ready for anything now.

"That was a big tiger," Clara said, relieved and a bit proud of herself.

"Yes it was," Marty said, feeling exactly the same way. This was an adventure they'd shared and survived, learning something about each other at the same time. The girl was tough; he knew that now. Clara stood up to the tiger without making a sound. He was certain she'd survive the loss of her mother and emerge stronger from the ordeal.

And Clara, for her part, knew that this stranger could be trusted, that he would protect her and comfort her as her own mother would.

They soon came to the sprawling shopping center that was the town square of Calabasas. People were bathing in the artificial pond on the corner, underneath the cracked, synthetic boulders of the fake, non-functioning waterfall and the sign advertising the center. Behind them, the giant Rolex had fallen and smashed into the parking lot.

When they rebuild this place, Marty thought, they should consider a Timex instead. It takes a licking and keeps on ticking, and it's probably a lot cheaper.

Marty, Clara, and Buck followed the street that sloped behind the center and rose into the hills, leading them finally to the red tiled guard house and iron gates of Oakridge Hills Estates.

If this had been a movie, Beth would have been waiting for him at the gates, crying with happiness. But it wasn't, and neither was she. It was too dark, and there were too many trees shrouding the steep hill, for Marty to see how badly hit the community was and to anticipate the odds of Beth being alive beyond those gates.

He would soon know, one way or the other.

There was a man standing behind the gate watching them approach. His hands were on his hips, right above the holstered gun clipped to the braided leather belt of his Ralph Lauren chinos. He wore the weapon like a man proud of his erection. He'd obviously been waiting all his life for a chance to strut around with it and he was going to enjoy every moment.

"That's close enough," the man held up his hand, motioning them to halt. "State your business."

"My business?" Marty asked incredulously, letting go of Clara's hand as he hobbled up to the gate. "I live here. Open the gate."

"I don't know you."

"I don't care. My name is Martin Slack, I live at 19067 Park Marbella and I want to go home. Now open the fucking gate."

"Do you know him, Walter?" The man turned to look at a balding man in a polo shirt and pleated shorts who was sitting on an icebox a few yards behind him.

"Nope," Walter replied. "Never seen him before, Bob."

Bob turned to Marty again. "I guess that settles it."

"Oh really?" Marty looked back at Buck. "Can you believe this guy?"

"You want me to handle this?" Buck asked.

"No, this is my home, Buck. I'll deal with it." Marty took another step towards the gate.

"I advise you to stay where you are," Bob said, letting his hand hover near his holster for emphasis. "This is a private community and these are desperate times. There are a lot of people who'd like to get in here right now and take advantage of our resources. So until order is restored, these gates are staying closed."

"I live here," Marty had enough of Bob. He looked at the bald guy on the curb. "Hey, Walter, go get my wife. Bob can watch me."

Walter got up, but Bob motioned him to stay. "Sit down, Walter." The bald guy did as he was told. Bob glared at Marty. "I got a better idea. Why don't you show me some ID?"

Yes, that was a good idea. In fact, it would have solved everything. The only trouble was, Marty didn't have it. He left it with the Plebneys and he knew Bob wasn't going to accept any explanations.

But Marty didn't come all this way, and go through so much, to let Bob stop him.

"Sure," Marty reached into his jacket for the ID he didn't have, pulled out his gun, and aimed it right at Bob's pudgy stomach. Bob made a lame move for his weapon.

"Go ahead, Bob, reach for your gun," Marty said. "By the time you undo the snap on your holster, you'll already be dead."

Bob swallowed hard and raised his hands.

Marty glanced at the bald guy. "I thought I told you to get my wife, Walter."

Walter nodded frantically and scrambled up the hill. Marty hoped the guy didn't have a heart attack before he reached their house.

"Now Bob, I want you to pull that holster off your belt and slide the gun under the gate to me before I shoot you just for being a prick."

Bob looked like he was going to cry. He hated parting with his gun, but he did as he was told, set the holstered gun on the ground, and gently kicked it under the gate. It slid to Marty's feet.

"Pick up the gun, Buck." Marty said.

Clara stepped forward hesitantly and reached for the gun.

"No, Clara. Don't touch that," Marty said. "Let Buck do it."

"I don't see him," she said.

Marty looked at her, then over his shoulder. There was no one there. Buck was gone.

"Where did Buck go?" Marty asked her. She stared back at him with a blank face. "Did he say anything to you?"

Clara shook her head. "He only talks to you."

"You're not right in the head, buddy," Bob said, his voice quavering. "Put the gun down before you hurt me or the little girl."

"Shut up," Marty looked down the barrel of his gun at Bob and became aware of the weapon in his hand for the first time.

Where did that come from?

With a trembling hand, he lifted his jacket and looked under his arm.

He was wearing a holster.

Which meant . . .

Marty quickly closed his jacket and checked his shoulder.

The gunshot wound wasn't there anymore.

Which meant . . .

He recognized the gun now. It belonged to Heller. It was a prop from the show he was visiting when the quake struck. Marty had the gun all along. And it was full of blanks.

Which meant . . .

Which meant all those times Buck was pitching himself as a series, talking about what a well-developed character he was, Marty was selling to himself.

Buck was already a character. A totally fictional one.

Buck did not exist. He never did.

"Oh my God," Marty muttered to himself, falling to his knees and closing his eyes, letting the gun fall to the ground.

No wonder Buck sounded just like that voice in his head. Buck was that voice in his head.

That Red Cross nurse was right, Marty thought, he did take a severe blow to the head. He'd been hallucinating for days.

His conscious mind tried to warn him, over and over again. Buck was one-dimensional. Buck's actions were clichés. It was impossible for Buck to survive the flood; it was an extraordinary contrivance that Buck found him impaled on that spike.

Why didn't he see that before? Why couldn't he accept it?

Because I needed Buck.

Without Buck pushing him, challenging him, forcing him to examine himself, he never would have survived. Marty had come to that realization long ago. Buck was there for Marty when he needed him and was gone when he didn't.

I've gone totally, completely insane, he thought. Maybe all of this is in my mind. I'm not even here. Maybe I'm still under my car, buried beneath a pile of bricks.

He was afraid to open his eyes. He didn't want to know the truth.

"Marty, oh my God, Marty."

It was Beth's voice. But was it real or, like Buck, a figment of his imagination?

He felt her arms around him, her tears on his cheek. "Please, Marty. Say something, are you all right?"

Slowly he lifted his head and opened his eyes.

Beth was on her knees in front of him, her lovely face, her adorable band of freckles, exactly as they were when he left her two days ago.

"I am now," he said.

She hugged him hard and he hugged her. They whispered, "I love you" again and again to each other. He would tell her all about his adventures and someday he might even tell her about Buck. Or maybe he'd just write about it instead.

Over her shoulder, he saw Clara standing there, a sad, lost look on her face. Marty gently pulled away from Beth. "Honey, I want you to meet Clara."

Beth turned, wiping the tears from her eyes, and looked at the girl for the first time. Maybe Beth saw the blue eyes and the freckles and also saw herself. Or maybe she just saw a frightened child.

"She's alone now," Marty said.

Beth reached out her arm to Clara. "No, she isn't."

Clara ran over and joined their hug.

Martin Slack was finally home.

AFTERWORD

Although I've lived in Los Angeles for over twenty years, survived the Northridge quake and the destruction of my home, and walked the route Marty traveled, I still referred to many books to add reality to my fantasy.

In particular, I am indebted to authors David Ritchie (*Superquake: Why Earthquakes Occur, and when the Big One Will Hit Southern California*), Mike Davis (*City of Quartz: Excavating the Future in Los Angeles,* and *Ecology of Fear: Los Angeles and the Imagination of Disaster*), Philip L. Fradkin (*Magnitude 8: Earthquakes and Life along the San Andreas Fault*), David Gebhard and Robert Winter (*Los Angeles: An Architectural Guide*), and Leonard Pitt and Dale Pitt (*Los Angeles: Encyclopedia of the City and County*) for their excellent studies and reference works.

All of the mistakes, geographical liberties, and scientific fudging are entirely my own.

Lee Goldberg

ABOUT THE AUTHOR

W riter/producer Lee Goldberg is a two-time Edgar Award nominee whose many TV credits include *Martial Law*, *Diagnosis Murder*, *Spenser: For Hire*, *Hunter Nero Wolfe*, and *Monk*. He's also the author of *My Gun Has Bullets*, *Beyond the Beyond*, *Man with the Iron-On Badge*, *Successful Television Writing* and the bestselling *Diagnosis Murder* and *Monk* series of original mystery novels.

Made in the USA
Lexington, KY
27 May 2011